YOUNG EZEKIEL
A LIFE OF LOVES

YOUNG EZEKIEL
A LIFE OF LOVES

JAMES THOMAS ANGELIDIS

Young Ezekiel:
A Life of Loves

James Thomas Angelidis
www.jtangelidis.com

First published by James Thomas Angelidis 2016.
This second edition published (as it appears in
Approaching the Kingdom: An Anthology)
by James Thomas Angelidis 2017.

Reprinted with no revisions to literature (second
edition) 2024.

Editorial Assistance:
Craig Cutler and Sharon Usdan Cutler.

Cover Design:
Layout by James Thomas Angelidis.

Cover Image:
Needlepoint by Angela Angelidis.
Photograph by James Thomas Angelidis.

Author Image:
(On author bio page) Photograph by Eddie Manso.

… Mustn't we, rather, look for those craftsmen whose good natural endowments make them able to track down the nature of what is fine and graceful, so that the young, dwelling as it were in a healthy place, will be benefited by everything; and from that place something of the fine works will strike their vision or their hearing, like a breeze bringing health from good places; and beginning in childhood, it will, without their awareness, with the fair speech lead them to likeness and friendship as well as accord?"

"In this way," he said, "they'd have by far the finest rearing."

- Plato, *The Republic*, Book III, 401c,
  Translation Allan Bloom

AUTHOR BIO

Raised next to New York City in Fort Lee, NJ, James Thomas Angelidis graduated from Boston University with a B.S. in Communication and a minor in Philosophy, from Montclair State University with a B.A. in Religious Studies and from Seton Hall University's Seminary with an M.A. in Theology. During his academic career, he merited awards, honors and the highest grades. After his first bachelor's degree, at the age of 24, he backpacked through Europe for 60 days and visited 28 cities in 11 countries - including France, Luxembourg, Belgium, Netherlands, Germany, Czech Republic, Austria, Switzerland, Italy, Spain and Portugal. For 9 years, he worked at Saint Basil Academy in Garrison, NY where he helped raise children with troubled backgrounds under the guiding light of the Greek Orthodox Christian Church. He spends his time spreading the teachings of his Lord and Savior Jesus Christ with his five books - *And the Lamb Spoke: Lessons from the Gospels* (ages 7-9), *Young Ezekiel: A Life of Loves* (young adults), *Writings* (young adults and adults), *In the Name of Salvation: Three Theological Treatises* (adults), *Approaching the Kingdom: An Anthology* (adults). You can find James's books on Amazon.com and BarnesAndNoble.com. James is online at www.jtangelidis.com, Instagram, Pinterest and LinkedIn.

ABOUT

I believe there is truth in the proverb, "The pen is mightier than the sword."

The damage done by the emperor's sword can be rectified by the writer's pen. Nothing can replace a life lost by the sword, but with the help of the pen, the story of that life can teach, inspire and unveil truth that can save many lives. When the emperor dies, so does his sword, as does his power and his influence on the world; yet, the writer's pen can leave a lasting impression unto the ages. The ideas behind the pen can change the world; something, the emperor tries to do with his sword, but inevitably fails. Certainly, if we dig deeper, we can discover additional meanings within the proverb's words, but it is clear that the pen is powerful. The pen can make a difference in people's lives and with the help of God, I hope to make a difference in people's lives with my pen. I hope to give life.

- James Thomas Angelidis

PREFACE

What is love?

Can you describe it?

Do you love your parents, friends, romantic partner and God in the same way?

In the English language, we use the word love in all these relationships, but the ancient Greeks - the first western philosophers - tried to capture, pinpoint and distinguish the different forms of love with four words: storge, philia, eros, agape.

In *Young Ezekiel: A Life of Loves*, Ezekiel will tell you about his life and loves. Though his life is unique, his relationships are like ours and, maybe, through his story, you will learn about yourself and the loves in your life.

YOUNG EZEKIEL
A LIFE OF LOVES

CONTENTS

YOUNG EZEKIEL
A LIFE OF LOVES

ONE

STORGE

My name is Ezekiel, which in Hebrew means God strengthens. My parents gave me that name because they believed it would protect me from harm. They believed in the power of a name. They believed it is important to know what a name means or where it comes from and to know who or what it honors. One's name is the beginning of one's identity in the world and represents one for life.

My parents loved me. It was love that was not wasted because it was love that nurtured my soul. Like fertile soil in a flower garden that strengths a lily's roots helping the flower to grow and bloom, their love was vital to my vitality. If I was well behaved or not, they loved me without condition because I was their son. I was not just any boy; I was their boy and that made me special. Their love made me feel that I had value, that they had me just so they could love me. They loved me without reservation, never held it back and would have done more, if it were possible. They praised me when I excelled, supported me when I failed and were patient with me when I struggled. They sacrificed money, time and pleasures to raise me. I'll never be able to repay them, but I loved them in return. Their love has given me confidence that I can do anything, that all things are possible. I was their only child and received their love undivided. I was the center of their lives and they were the center of mine. I was their heart and they were mine. I remember mother squeezing me for no reason other than because she loved me. My parents cherished every moment that was a first and understood how precious life is. They bronzed my first shoes, recorded my first words and videotaped my first steps. Pictures captured our experiences. Some of my favorite images are the candid ones because they are natural and honest. They have no disguise and not one fails to depict our love for each other. I have no bad memories of them. They provided me with food, shelter and love. I lacked nothing.

Born off the coast of Florida on a small island called Omorfi, I reminisce most about my days on the beach. The walk to the beach was just as much fun as being at the beach. When I was a tot, father would carry me on his shoulders. They made the perfect seat as if shoulders were meant to be sat upon and provided a fantastic view that was superior to what I was accustomed to because of my short height. For those moments, I was a giant and felt indomitable. No one was taller than me, I felt. As tall as the trees,

I would reach high to grab a leaf for no reason other than because I could. It was my natural inclination to a special situation. There was one time when I tested my capacity's limits, stretched for a leaf and almost fell. However, father did not let that happen. He maintained his balance and compensated for my childish behavior. He had it all under control. He could have scolded me because I could have hurt myself, but instead, he said, "Ezekiel, my son, be careful. I need you, just as much as you need me. If you fall, you could get hurt and that would hurt me." I never forgot my father's words because they taught me that our love for each other made us one and that we were an extension of each other. We had to love and take care of ourselves, not just for ourselves, but also for each other. I know now that if I fell and got hurt, it would have hurt father emotionally, just as much as it would have hurt me physically. Perhaps, even more. His love for me was beyond sympathy or empathy. He would have died for me because my life was more important to him than his own life.

I remember walking in between father and mother and they would swing me with their arms as I held their hands. In the middle of the air, I felt as though I was floating and during that climax, time seemed to stand still. I would hold my breath, my heart would pause and my smile would beam from joy. "Again, again," I would yell and they fulfilled my request without a thought. They would do anything to make me happy. As I grew a bit and got too big to swing from their arms, other games followed. Sometimes, we would kick stones and see how long we could keep one in front of us. I would pass it to mother and she would pass it to father. Our play evolved. Even though the games changed, fun never did. It kept us young. Each of their inner child resurfaced when we played together. They humbled themselves to my level and for those moments, I was their equal.

The beach was a ten minute walk away from home. On the way, we would pass a pasture on the left of the road enclosed by an old weathered wooden fence. A dark red barn with white trim overlooked the pasture, which was made up of gold tinted grass. Cattle roamed the field and they would feed on the grass slowly and carefree. Sometimes, a cow would take a break, look at us and moo and I would wonder what the cow was thinking. Was he trying to say hello or were we interrupting his mealtime? I could also hear the restless chickens heckling in their coop and a couple of dogs replying to their calls. It was the same scene every time we traveled by and because of the expectation of the situation, I was never surprised or let down. The pasture was like a part of my home and I felt I could claim it as my own, but that is what children do. They take possession of the things they are most fond of. It is not their fault because they lack maturity. Unfortunately, some people never grow up and learn to share. It takes a well-adjusted and well-balanced mind to play with others. Some people maintain a selfish and audacious attitude and wars are fought because of such people. Treasures and territory are what they desire and they fail to love their neighbor, which is humankind's second greatest sin after failing to love God.

The beach bustled with activity. Children yelling, water splashing and music playing pulsated through the air. Frisbee throwing, water surfing and volleyball bumping energized the scene. The tourists responded to this the most, but father, mother and I took an unbeaten path known only by the locals. We entered the beach with everyone else, but around a picketed fence, some beach grass and a curiously massive boulder was a coastal strip that was a living dream. The energy was exciting, but a bit much. Father, mother and I preferred serenity over the commotion. Our neighbors frequented it and so did a couple of my schoolmates and their parents. The white unstained sand made the water look blue as it mirrored the color of the blue sky. I could see, beneath the transparent water, the stones and coral that rested on the bottom of the ocean. Every time I saw that sight my natural inclination was to jump in. I would jet to the water and with each step, I would kick up sand behind me. During those hot days, the water refreshed my tanned skin and once I took my first dip, I could stay in there for over an hour. My parents would joke that in a previous life I must have been a fish, even though, I would swim paddling my arms and legs like a puppy dog. While I joined my friends in the water, my parents laid out our beach towels with our belongings by the sand dunes. In mother's bag were suntan lotion, house keys, money and a couple of books. Father carried the cooler stored with baby carrots, cucumbers, cheese and tomato sandwiches with a little mayonnaise and some fresh water. By the time they settled in and got comfortable, I would take a break from playing and mother would see me approach them and ask, "Is my son hungry?" I always nodded my head yes. She knew me better than anyone else; I rarely had to say a word for her to know what I was thinking. Then, we would make a picnic and have our own private party. We would huddle together sitting cross legged on our beach towels with the food in front of us. Sometimes, mother would toss a baby carrot in the air toward father. She would direct it toward his mouth and father would follow, catch, chew and enjoy. Mother would toss them just right and father always caught them. Then, they would look at each other, smile and give each other high-fives for jobs well done. I would laugh and get high-fives, too, because I was their son. As I got older, I would imitate father and soon enough we were all laughing. It was not that we did not want others' company. We just did not need anyone else to have a good time. All we needed was each other.

As the day passed, father, mother and I would gravitate to the water's edge and sit there while the water washed over our legs. The gentle sweeping waves tingled our skin and calmed our spirits. This tranquil massage will put anyone in a good mood. As we lounged there, father and I often built drip castles out of the wet sand. The powder-like white sand morphed into a mud-like brown when the water touched it. The small grainy consistency was rough, yet smooth - perfect for drip castles. We would grab a fistful of wet sand and guide it off our fingers, so it would drip to the ground where it would accumulate creating the tower of a castle. It was a simple trick that produced an elegant result. The castles resembled 19th century Spanish architect Antoni Gaudi's basilica, "Sagrada Familia." We also filled the plastic cups we brought for our drinking water with wet sand, so we could build miniature forts. The key is to not use dry sand that will crumble or water saturated sand that will get stuck in the cup; but, rather, a consistency in between the two. We would stack one fort or drip castle on top of other forts fashioning many tall structures that were grouped together creating a kingdom. Our kingdom would remain until the water attacked it. Nature's power is mightier than anything humankind can make, even with our overconfident arrogance. Other times, father, mother and I would dig massive pits. We would dig so deep that at the bottom, we would hit water. The first time this happened, I was puzzled. Father told me that if we dig deeper, we would reach the other side of the earth. I paused with my eyes in a daze contemplating the idea. When I got stuck on the thought, father confessed he was teasing me and then smiled, grabbed my neck and kissed my forehead. Sometimes, mother and I could convince father to get into the pit, so we could bury him up to the neck and all we could see is his head above the ground. More often than not, he did not mind looking silly for his family in front of others and that is what made him cool. Silly is not really silly when love is involved.

Father also showed me how to skip rocks on the surface of the ocean. He was much more coordinated than I. When he threw the rock upon the ocean, it would skip five or six times. When I threw the rock, it would hit kerplunk then fall to the bottom. The trick was to find a flat and smooth rock and direct the throw to the surface of the water. I can do it now the way father did it then, but when I was a child, it was like magic. Another favorite pastime at the beach was looking for sea glass - glass made smooth by years of being tossed around in the sand and sea - on the beach. Mother learned this pastime from her mother and passed it down to me. The beach coast was long. It would take most people twenty-five minutes to walk along it and another twenty-five minutes to walk back, but for mother and I and other sea glass enthusiasts, the full walk could exceed two hours and we enjoyed every minute. The sea glass would settle on the shore beside the pebbles, but the colors of the sea glass would pop and glisten in the sunlight. Browns, greens and whites were common, but rare colors like purple were always prized. During the day, I would carry my favorite pieces in my pocket as good luck charms and at night, I would keep them on my stand by my bed so they would always be near me.

During the weekdays, father worked as a teacher in the town high school. He taught eleventh grade history. He was most fascinated with the American Civil War and legacy of President Abraham Lincoln. He was father's hero. Wisdom, truth and honor are words that father used to describe him to me when I was a child. He used Lincoln to put a face on virtue and integrity that would help mold my character. That was his way of planting a seed in my mind, so I too would strive to be great and make this world a better place.

He explained to me that Lincoln was an avid reader. Lincoln grew up in the American frontier where skills with an axe and hunting were prized, not education. Most children who grew up like him found no value in books because their parents did not find them important, but Lincoln was an exception. Though tall and strong, he had dreams beyond the frontier and he believed that reading would make his dreams a reality. And, when most boys were idling away time, Lincoln was reading diligently. During the summer, he would read outside and at night, he would read under a lamp. He was curious, read with tenacity and reveled in the acquisition of knowledge. At first, Lincoln read because he enjoyed the written word, but as he matured, he realized its greater value.

Books were hard to find in the frontier, but most homes had a Bible. Lincoln read and reread the Bible, memorized large portions of it and could recite them by heart, particularly the Psalms. Though not a church-going Christian, he took Scripture seriously and lived by its principles. During one cold night, he saw a defeated drunk man lying in the road and, without thought, helped the man to his feet, got him into a warm home and cared for him the next day. He was acting like the Good Samaritan who Jesus preached. He believed in God, but was skeptical about miracles and transcendence. The *Dilworth's Speller* was another popular book that Lincoln had access to which taught wisdom lessons that guided him through his youth. It encouraged reading to enhance the self and introduced him to literature outside the Bible, such as Aesop's fables, which became favorites with their sagacity. *Pilgrim's Progress* was another important book that directed his moral compass. He read anything and everything, including biographies, histories, novels and poetry. In fact, he wrote fine poetry himself. He recorded his favorite literature in a journal - a practice that strengthened his later writings and speeches. He absorbed and savored Shakespeare's works, which gave him greater insight into and a more complete perspective of human nature. He was different than most boys and by the time he was nineteen, he had an idea that he would be a great man. Father explained this to me as well as to his students who would soon be off to college where they would discover their potential. He made us believe that, like Lincoln, we could be great if we worked hard and pursued knowledge and wisdom.

Father believed in his profession, in cultivating the young minds of his students who will one day shape the world. He understood he may not make history, but he taught his students that one day they could. He believed inspiration is divine and transformative. It prompts people to act and if it remains, extraordinary things will happen. It is like supernatural motivation. It is a thought that ignites a flame in a person that has the potential to set a group and nation to rise and make change happen.

Father did not make a lot of money and we were not rich, but father was doing what he loved and that love came home with him every night. Some people toil day and day to make money, but are miserable. Money can enhance quality of life, but it is no guarantee of happiness. Father found a healthy balance that few people do. He believed that studying history was noble. He used to recite this one proverb, his favorite, to me by 19th century Spanish American philosopher and writer George Santayana, "Those who cannot remember the past are condemned to repeat it." So, we have a responsibility in this world to be knowledgeable of who we are and what we have done and to be aware of our capabilities - both good and bad - so we can make this world a better place for our children and our grandchildren and so on. Only by knowing history can one change history and prevent the mistakes of the past. 5th century BC Greek philosopher Socrates lived by the ancient Greek aphorism, "Know thyself." This piece of wisdom was the beginning of Western philosophy. Self-knowledge helps one to know one's strengths and weaknesses to make one a better person. One has to examine his own life and history, so he can make better decisions for himself and excel. Santayana's aphorism has roots in the ancient Greek aphorism. They both speak truth about awareness and transformation - one for the individual and the other for humankind.

Another of father's favorite proverbs is from 1st century BC Roman historian Titus Livy who said, "We fear things in proportion to our ignorance of them." The more we know about something, the less there is to fear. Most of us fear the unknown because we are unable to see the next step in the darkness of uncertainty. With knowledge, we become familiar with our surroundings and can confidently take the next step. Familiarity leads to comfort and security. It makes learning possible and prejudice fade. Father always encouraged me to explore and seek out answers to my questions. He taught me the value of books. Mother, too, was well read and, every so often, we would go together as a family to book fairs to buy used books - so much fun.

The school father taught at was a ten minute walk away from our home. Mother would prepare lunch for him and we would walk together to his school to deliver it to him. He would tell us that seeing us was the best part of his day. Mother and I were just as happy to see him.

Before I attended school and mother returned to work, I would spend the weekdays with her. She was a nurse, but chose to leave her occupation to raise me. She and father spoke about expenses and priorities and they decided to sacrifice many of the material pleasures that occupy many. Those days she spent with me are priceless. No money could replace their worth. As a child, I went to sleep early and woke up early and mother was always there. She bathed me, fed me and read to me. We were friends, but she was my mother first. She did not let me get away with misbehavior. If I made a mess of my room, I had to clean it otherwise mother would take away my favorite toys until I learned the lesson about the privilege of possessions. I was disciplined and learned right from wrong from her, but her actions always conveyed love. Few things were as satisfying as her smile and praise. She taught me about how to grow up strong in this world. If I tripped and fell, she gave me the opportunity to pick myself up, but if I hurt myself, she was there to comfort me with her embrace. In the playground, she gave me enough distance to wander around, so I could explore and learn independently. She let me make mistakes, so I could learn from them. If I tried climbing up some apparatus and could not, I learned my capabilities and limitations. In the local playground is where I learned how to interact with strangers, make friends and share. She showed me how to look for the humanity in people. I was sensitive to myself and others and developed the quality of compassion at a young age. I would see children cry or have temper tantrums and look at them with concern wondering why they were upset. Respect is the foundation for a civil society and as I interacted with other children, mother helped mold my character and behavior. I realized sharing was how to make friends. It leads to a peaceful and joyful relationship, but if a child stole my toy, I expressed my distress and often hollered at or chased after them. Mother understood the dangers of strangers, but did not smother or shelter me. I learned quickly from her guidance. For example, when I was around three years old and beginning to verbalize my thoughts, I introduced myself to an older woman and said, "Hello. My name is Ezekiel." And she said, "Nice to meet you Ezekiel. That's a lovely name." I said "I am three. I can count to ten." The woman must have thought this was very cute and she engaged me in conversation. I thought I was a big boy and was proud to express myself, but looking back, this could have been dangerous. For a child, talking to strangers is usually not a good idea. I was not cognizant of it at the time, but in retrospect, I realize mother was there overseeing this interaction and was there to protect me. I was learning about myself and how to communicate under mother's watch.

Behavior modification was important, but fun was the reason we came to the playground. Swings, slides and the jungle gym created a universe of unlimited possibilities. Always excited to visit, I never got bored of the playground. Yelling, laughing and running were common practice. Playing got me tired, so I could sleep soundly, which was good for me, but good for mother, too. It gave her time to gather her thoughts and rest. Being a good mother can be exhausting, but through her hugs and kisses, I know there was little else that she would rather do. She prepared me for preschool and a life beyond our nuclear family. When I began school, she returned to work as a nurse.

Raising a child is the toughest job in the world. To every child, mother is most important. Everyone says his or her mother is the best. Even in his song "Dear Mama," rapper Tupac Shakur praises his mother, a woman many would criticize. It's a deep and sensitive song from a self-proclaimed ghetto thug. Tupac Shakur and I grew up very differently, but I can relate to his song because I have the same love for my mother as he did for his mother. I do not know what it is about mothers. I am not a mother. Where do they get their love? Is it innate? Though often overlooked and taken for granted, no job is more serious and important. Mothers and fathers are responsible for another human being who will one day be a part of society: fact. Will that child be a cancer to the world or bright light? Most of that has to do with the parents. Monsters and saints are rare, but parents have the obligation to raise a child who will contribute to society; otherwise, they will have done an injustice to the child and society. There is no such thing as a perfect parent, just as there is no such thing as a perfect human being. However, if you love your child and raise your child with God and Christ, you will have done your best and what is expected of you by God.

We lived in a modest one story white painted wood shingled house. Sky blue wood shutters bordered the sides of the windows and we had a matching front sky blue door that accented our home's cozy appearance. There were trimmed bushes in front of the house that had spectacular lemon yellow lilies living below. To the side was a stone birdbath that was frequented by a family of green and yellow colored parakeets with mixed black and white wings. Butterflies befriended them and together they filled the air with compassion. The dainty birds and butterflies were easily flustered and every time I approached them they would flutter away. A palm tree proudly peered over our house enjoying the horizon. A confident, spirited and free American flag swayed in the wind on a pole. Meandering through our green grass was a path made up of smooth beach stones that lead to the front door. On the side of our house was a studio apartment that was once a garage. Our tenant was a fisherman and crew member on one of the island's party boats that catered to the tourists who wanted an adventure at sea and to catch a few fish. He was middle aged with a scruffy beard and had no family of his own. He was a bit of a wanderer and loner, but settled down in Omorfi. We did not spend much time with him, but he was respectful and paid his rent promptly. Father's salary was our primary source of income, but the monthly rent paycheck helped a lot with our expenses and alleviated some pressure for father and mother.

After entering through the front door, one would find a rather large open furnished room with beige short looped durable carpet introducing the inside of the house. There was a mat next to the door where we would place our sandals and shoes, so we would minimize sand and dirt from entering in the house. There was also a coatrack where we would keep our coats and umbrellas that we would use depending on the weather. Spread out, yet carefully positioned clay potted green plants added warmth and life to the atmosphere. Mother and I would water them daily and as I got older, I would do so on my own. For this and other chores, like throwing out the garbage, I would get paid a weekly allowance that showed me responsibility and the reward of work. The walls were adorned with mother's paintings. She painted for pleasure and often imitated her favorite artist, 19th century French Impressionist painter Claude Monet. She would paint in the spacious entrance room sitting in front of an easel. There was usually light music playing in the background. She was very focused, yet at peace. It was like meditation for her. She tried to paint every day and I knew how to keep myself busy by reading, drawing or playing in the backyard, so she could. When she was finished for the day, she would neatly place her work and materials in the corner to the right of the entrance room's front door. This way it was not visible when introduced to the inside of the house. Our house was not very big and the open room was the best place to paint. Two cork colored couches in the far corner of the room leaned against the walls and an oval glass coffee table conveniently sat in front of them. Mother left cashews and almonds in a bowl on the coffee table in case we wanted a little something to nibble on and as a light treat for any guests. Usually open, the windows brought in fresh air and the ceiling fan helped circulate it.

The most mystical room in the house was the family study room. The floor was wood and three walls were painted white. The fourth wall and the high ceiling were made up of sun windows, so the room was always lit with natural light. It also allowed for a spectacular and tranquil view of the ocean and the sunset. At the square room's center was a square off-white flokati rug with a circular wood coffee table on it. The table was surrounded by three brown leather seats with jade tree plants separating them. There were four small, yet powerful speakers stationed in each corner of the room, so if you sat on one of the seats you would be immersed in musical sounds of mostly classical, jazz, rock or hip-hop. On the walls were framed prints of Gandhi, Mother Teresa and Lincoln, as well as framed prints of Van Gogh, Matisse and Monet paintings. Below the prints stood wood bookshelves that bordered the room and they were filled with father's history books and classics of literature, mother's art and photography books and my children's books. My favorite books were of the Berenstain Bears series. They taught Christian lessons with engaging pictures without being overtly religious. I found the collection of Aesop's fables fascinating and it - with father and mother's commentaries - made me think deeply at an early age. I had a great affinity for picture books, particularly those of dinosaurs. Their bones and muscles and the mystery of their life and extinction spurred my imagination to wander. In the study room on the floor or in my seat, I used draw and color pictures of them and other animals with careful detail. I tried to copy their images as realistically as possible. Mother and father posted my best artwork on the walls with their prints. When they put them up, I stood taller with my shoulders back and chest high. I pledged allegiance to hard work. Few moments were as rewarding as when my parents hung my work on the wall.

Mother's passion for art extended beyond the modern masters' works to include Orthodox Christian Byzantine icons. Her passion influenced father and they developed a common devotion to the icons.

Mother's love of art and father's belief in inspiration embodied by his heroes seemed to wed well in the icons. Father and mother placed icons of Christ Jesus and the Virgin Mother Mary in their bedroom and mine, too, on top of our bureaus leaning against the wall. The portraits were authentic paintings about the size of a book cover. They carried more than an esthetic appeal - they were there to protect us. My parents were not kooky and their beliefs had nothing to do with superstition, but rather a deep belief in the supernatural and the men and women who embodied it. This same philosophy was applied when they named me. It was given to me to protect me from harm. An icon of the Prophet Ezekiel hung on the wall inside my bedroom next to the door above the light switch to remind me every time I came in and out of the room that my name had a source. It had meaning and was fundamental to my identity. I did not like it as a child because I thought it was weird and felt I had to explain its meaning when I introduced myself to others; however, today, I say it with pride because its uniqueness reminds me of my parents who believed in its value.

When I was very little, mother played a lot of classical music in our home. She learned somewhere that classical music helped the mind grow intellectually. She believed that the way fruits and vegetables were good for the body, classical music was good for the mind. Each provides nutrients that foster good health. She preferred Bach above the other classical musicians because much of his music was Christian oriented and mother wanted to nourish me with as much positive as possible. My parents had eclectic musical tastes. More often than not, jazz played in our study. The type of jazz they listened to varied, but it usually did not have words, which can be distracting if one is reading and trying to concentrate. Jazz seems to help the mind process reading material because it helps the mind flow with the ideas. Like classical, jazz is intellectual, but also spiritual. John Coltrane's music is a perfect example. From its birth, jazz has had soul in it. The artist's honesty and nakedness while performing his piece makes it impossible to not come from the soul. Coltrane, though, elevated jazz's spiritual possibilities and brought that soulful quality to the forefront. His album *A Love Supreme* ends with his track, "Psalm" - praising God's Supreme Love for us. The album is not a peaceful expression, rather an exuberant excitement of devotion to God. It's a piece of art that stands alone, that demands attention, that leaves an impression. We did not listen to Coltrane's *A Love Supreme* while we were reading - it is too intense - but I mention it here to highlight jazz's spiritual nature. Albums like Miles Davis's *Kind of Blue* we played regularly while we were reading in the study because they are soft and subtle. My parents enjoyed the masters of all the popular genres of American music. They were astute and musically knowledgeable. Listening to music was how father and mother spent their alone time together. I remember falling asleep and hearing them listening to music in the entrance room. It was spacious and father and mother would dance together. I know this because more than once I woke up from sleep and walked into the entrance room looking for father and mother and found them dancing. The first time this happened, I was startled because I did not expect it. But, when I saw the activity, it looked like fun and I wanted to join them. Father and mother smiled at me, but swiftly, yet calmly escorted me back to my bedroom. I quickly learned that it was not my playtime. It was their playtime. Music is the strongest medium that speaks to the soul. Books, at their best, teach us about the human condition, but music has the power to amplify or change our condition within an hour depending on what we need. There is always a song that we can connect with no matter what mood we are in. It might be because of the lyrics, the melodies or the rhythms that make us feel alive. It's more than sound because it is an expression of the human spirit. A talented musician is acutely in tune to what is inside of him and creates to share that with his audience. Sometimes, it is so personal that he may not want others hear his music, but if he does and it resonates with others, few things are as unifying. He is a kindred spirit that can hear what is inside of you and speaks for you. Few things can bring people together the way a good song does. Music is the most potent art form. Within seconds, a good song can reach the soul; however, it is the most fleeting art form. It changes with the times. It's like a flashing spark of light that excites, but disappears as quickly as it appeared. On the other hand, books are the most enduring art form. Homer wrote the *Iliad* and the *Odyssey* around 2800 years ago and it still lives, stirs the human spirit and speaks to the soul. As readers today, we can benefit from the wisdom of the people who lived before us. Books make learning about the world, humanity and oneself possible and more complete. And, the best have the potential to pass the test of time, which is the most demanding and authoritative test I know. Both books and music reflect the human condition, but touch us in different ways: music is more emotional, while books are more cerebral.

We lived in the town of Paidi in Omorfi. It was more like the size of a village than a suburb. The roads were narrow, but accommodated for two way traffic. Most of the buildings were one or two stories tall. The houses were not cramped. They had space to breathe, but were close enough and neighbors were comfortable enough that one neighbor could ask another - without strain or reservation - for a cup of sugar. Our house was closer to the beach than the center of town. There were many beaches around Paidi, but we could walk to the beach we frequented. We had to drive a couple of minutes to get to the center of town where there was a large traffic circle that had a gazebo in the middle. It was the landmark everyone referred to when someone needed directions. The traffic circle brought everything in town close together and easy to get to. The locals owned and operated the shops and restaurants. Corporations and franchises had not tainted the setting. The pizza shop was always busy and for good reason because I do not know any person who does not like pizza. Motels as opposed to resort type hotels catered to the tourists. Paidi had a reputation of being a getaway destination. Visitors escaped the busy bedlam of cities to relax. There was no nightlife to attract party people, which is why families gravitated toward it. The miniature golf course called Putt Paradise, which had a tropical theme, and the ice cream house called Cow's Delight, which was painted with a cow like black and white pattern, stood side by side and were very popular. Once or twice a year, father, mother and I would join the tourists for an evening of fun. The miniature golf course was well lit, so you could putt even when the day turned into night. It had nine holes, with a special tenth hole that was elevated above the ground and was inside a large shark's mouth. There was a little ramp and if you hit the ball with a single stroke with the right amount of accuracy and speed, it would coast off the ramp through the air into the hole and you would win a baseball cap with the Putt Paradise logo, which was good business and good advertising. Mother owned that hole. Father and I never won a hat, but mother won two. She would wear them like crowns in our house touting her royalty status and what could father and I say? Very little. She was the queen.

Yard sales were plentiful in Paidi. Mother and I could spend hours hunting for bargains. The old adage, "One man's trash is another man's treasure" carries truth. For a couple of dollars, I bought a snorkeling mask that I used for years. I guess the owner no longer needed it and getting rid of it for a couple of dollars was worth it. That was okay with me. The seller and I both won. My best purchase was a fishing rod and reel I bought for father for Father's Day. Mother saw the set first and then called me over. It was brand new and was being sold for a quarter of the price it was marketed for in stores. Our timing was good because someone else could have easily picked it up before us. We got lucky. Few things are as satisfying as a good deal. It was a perfect gift because father and I would go fishing together on his days off from work, so I knew he would like it. To go fishing, we would walk fifteen minutes from our house along the boat dock boardwalk to our spot near the main docking station. On our way, we would stop at the bait and tackle shop that was next to the fishing party boats. We would pick up a dozen claims, our preferred bait for flounder, our desired catch. Lures in plastic transparent packages hung on the shop's wall. Their shimmers appealed to my eyes. Silver, green and yellow glistened in the light, but the lures were costly. Father stuck with the claims because that was what worked for him. They came in a re-sealable bag and father temporarily stored them in our five gallon white plastic paint bucket that he carried. I carried the small tackle box where we kept fishing line, hooks, weights and other standard equipment. He held his rod and reel and I held mine. We would spend hours fishing and fill our ocean water filled paint bucket with our catch. Tourists would wander through the dock, stumble across us and wow at our bucket of fish. "What kind of fish are those? How many fish is that? What kind of bait are you using? How long have you been here?" were common questions. I answered every question without hesitation because I was proud of our accomplishment. When the day was done, we usually caught dozens of fish, gut and cleaned them on the dock and then brought them home to mother who would fry them up for dinner that night. It was gratifying to work and eat the fruits of our labor. One day, we decided to try something new and board one of the fishing party boats. I had never been on a boat before. I had been waiting for this day all week, got up early that day and had some breakfast. We walked to the dock then got in line to enter the boat. The hair on my arms stood with anticipation and excitement. We stepped in and claimed our spots. The sun was hot that day and in the air was a wind. As the boat got out into the ocean, the waves were beating against its sides. Choppy waters were not a part of our agenda, but we had no choice other than to move on.

About twenty minutes into our trip, as I was leaning against the boat's edge with my pole in hand and line out, I got dizzy, light headed, weak in the knees and my stomach started to turn. I glanced to my side and noticed other guys with the same symptoms. Then, one guy upchucked his breakfast. Then, a second, third and fourth. It was contagious, like an epidemic, from one man to the next. I could not hold it in any longer and succumbed to my illness and upchucked along with them. This continued for the remainder of the trip, which lasted for four and a half grueling hours. I would take breaks from emptying my stomach by lying down groaning on a bench. The merciless waves defeated me that day. That was it. Never again. I learned my lesson. From that day on, I stayed on the dock.

During the day, mother would take me around town as she ran her errands. The post office, laundromat and corner convenience store were regular destinations. The doctor's office was another familiar place where I would get routine checkups. Most of the time, I followed mother dragging my feet. Going to all these places felt like work. I would rather be home playing with my toys. However, I did not mind our weekly trip to the grocery mart.

The only one in town, the grocery mart was owned and operated by our neighbors and we looked forward to seeing them every time we went shopping. Their three children were older than me and helped stock shelves and work the registers. You can make a lot of money owning your own business, but in can be a lot of work because its success depends on you. You reap what you sow. However, even with hard work, success is not guaranteed. As with everything, God's Grace is pivotal. I remember it being built, so it was relatively new to the community and outsold other specialty food stores because it carried most products and produce. Though not the size of a chain establishment, it had its own bakery, deli and fish market inside. Upon walking through the front entrance, I could smell the scent of fresh fish. Since we lived by the ocean, the stock of fish was replenished daily, so the smell was brisk, not spoiled, as it is in some places. We always picked up the staples - like milk and eggs - and took advantage of the in-store bakery and deli.

My parents were frugal and conservative with money, but not cheap, particularly with food. Any extra money was usually spent to make a good meal. Mother did not hesitate to buy steaks, as long as they were on sale. Good food enhanced the quality of our lives and was something we enjoyed together. Dinner was a formal, yet informal event. We sat together at 6:30 every evening, set the table and said prayer. Food followed and as we spoke about our days, we tended to let loose and indulge in each other's company. New stories as well as old stories about our lives surfaced in dialogue in a way that defines family. Dinnertime was the climax of our day. There was nothing else we would rather do, no place we would rather be and no others on earth who we would rather be with. Mother made a lot of soup, father's choice meal. If father had a long day at work and mother cooked some soup, he would spontaneously brighten up. Chicken noodle, split pea and Cajun shrimp were among the regular dishes. And, if we had a few extra ingredients that seemed to go together, mother would put them together and make some gumbo. She mixed up the menu, so father was always surprised.

In the grocery mart, mother would play question/answer games with me to keep me from causing mischief, which worked, at least, temporarily. She would ask, "What does organic mean?" or "What is poultry?" The questions were not always easy, but I liked the process of learning. When I learned that tomatoes are botanically defined as fruit and not as vegetables, my mind nearly exploded. Chefs may use the savory, unsweet tomato as a vegetable in cooking, but the tomato is the fleshy seed-bearing body of a flowering plant, which makes it a fruit. It is not the root, stem or leaf of a plant, which would make it a vegetable.

For me, our trip to the grocery mart was an adventure that began when we chose our grocery cart. They were large - much bigger than I was - and the key was to find one that had strong wheels - this way it could support my weight as I treated it like my own private chariot. When I was small, I would sit in the cart with the groceries, but when I got bigger and started to crush the groceries, I would stand outside on the front axle and hang onto to the body. Mother was the driver and I was the passenger. It was thrilling and unpredictable because I rode blind with my back in front. It was the only way to grasp the cart. I never knew which direction mother would be pushing. "Faster, faster," I would shout, but mother would tell me to pipe down. I would comply, so she would not got tired of me and kick me off. The ride would freeze when mother stopped the cart to pick up food from the shelves. This gave me the opportunity to run around. With mother busy, I had the freedom to play in the aisle. I would run up the aisle and half way through I would drop to the side of my butt and slide. The faster I ran, the further I would slide. Then, I would run down the aisle and do it again. I did this as long as mother was searching and reaching for the shelved food. This could last minutes and I would slide a half a dozen times. I perfected the skill and considered myself an athlete. I felt like the grocery mart aisle sliding Olympic champion and the other customers were the crowd mesmerized by my athletic excellence. I could hear them chanting my name, "Ezekiel! Ezekiel! Ezekiel!" even if it was only in my imagination. When mother moved on to the next item on her shopping list and restarted the chariot, I would get back on board and the games would continue. Mother would not get angry at me because she was expecting it, but if I was getting too loud and disrupting the other customers, she would give me a look and I would stop because I knew if I did not, I would be in trouble. That look was more powerful than any words she could say and I knew exactly what she meant. If I was relatively well behaved and not disrupting the other customers too much, she would allow me choose a candy. I always picked a chocolate. It could be dark chocolate, milk chocolate, with peanut butter or coconut - it did not matter. I would savor the taste because it was my favorite food.

When I was little, every day was special and every Saturday morning was like a holiday. On Saturdays, I would wake up early without any outside notice - only from my exuberant spirit that could barely wait to begin the day. Slowly, my eyes would open and a smile would break through from within and surface onto my face. I would take a deep breath and inhale the sunlit air that filled my bedroom and yawn a great yawn to fight drowsiness's gravity, which wanted to keep me under the sheets. I would stretch my body straight from the curl it kept itself in during the night, feeling my blood flow through my veins, regenerating my muscles. The light outdoor breeze would strike the palm tree's leaves, which in turn would break the wind. I could hear the confrontation of nature's elements, which seemed to encourage me to get out of bed. I could hear the birds chime into nature's rhythmic commotion and sometimes a bird would peep through the window and chirp hello. My spirit and nature seemed to start the day together and begin the first page of the day's chapter unified. I would savor the surreal quality of my dreams and dance with it until my mind's eye lit out the cloudiness of unreality and dusted off sleep's final phase.

After I broke free from my bed sheets, I would hurry into father and mother's adjacent room and slip into their bed. They would try to sleep into a couple extra dream sequences, but I was too excited to be awake to let that happen. I would cocoon myself in between them as if I was about to go back to sleep, but my restlessness kept my eyes wide open. I can still smell the fresh scent and feel the soft texture of father and mother's newly laundered pillowcases and bed sheets. When mother caressed my cheek with her hand and father brushed my hair with his hand, I knew they, too, were ready to rise and shine. It was the only morning in the week that father and mother would remain in bed later than I. Father did not have work and we usually had no plans, so Saturday mornings were just for us with no distraction from the outside world. We would lovingly give each other butterfly kisses - eyelash kisses on the cheek. It would tickle, but that was how we greeted each other on Saturday mornings. We would also snuggle up together and sing songs. Sometimes they were commercially successful songs and other times we made up our own lyrics to random melodies and beats that popped into our heads, but whatever we sang was always a happy tune about us being together.

Father would get up and walk to the two bedroom windows and slide the window curtains to the side to let the sunlight in. At that moment, I could see the sunrays break into the room through the transparent windows dividing the light and darkness in front of me. Dust particles drifted through the sunlit air and never seemed to land on anything, but rather floated effortlessly continuously harmoniously silently within the sun's rays. One at a time, we would enter the bathroom to scrub our faces and brush our teeth. By then, it would be about half past nine and our taste buds and stomachs would alert us that it was time for breakfast. Mother would cook. She was a genius in the kitchen. Everything she made was good and the meals were as healthy as possible without losing flavor. I can still taste her homemade whole-wheat pancakes. We would dress the pancakes with cottage cheese and maple syrup and have some fresh fruit and a glass of orange juice on the side. As she was cooking, father and I would prepare the table. We were a team in that kitchen and we savored not only the food, but also each other's company. When we finished eating, father and I would clean up the kitchen and put the dishes away while mother put the leftovers in the refrigerator, so we could enjoy them the next day. For the rest of Saturday, we would be at the beach - swimming, building drip castles, skipping rocks on the surface of the water and looking for sea glass.

Sundays were reserved for spiritual renewal.

My parents did not follow an organized religion, but they believed in the Almighty God of the three great monotheistic world religions - Judaism, Christianity and Islam. They believed He is a Supreme Presence who plays a role in people's lives and that He is Powerful. Most people in the world believe in God and some do not and my parents felt bad for those who do not. Some people deny the existence of God through science. The reasoning mind and the senses are the foundation of science; however, my parents knew that the reasoning mind and the senses are not trustworthy. My parents recognized that science has achieved great things and that it has taught us much from the microscopic to the cosmic. And, they believed in the noble honesty of the scientific method and it's longing for truth to the point of confession of its limitations never knowing if its findings are completely correct. Conclusions are constantly being reassessed by means of new tests and discoveries. Science has not given us all the answers. And, it may never. With science, there is no end in sight. There will always be new realms to explore and more questions to ask. Science desires to see the whole iceberg even though, more often than not, it is only a witness of the iceberg's tip. Plato understood this and allegorized the weakness of perception in his allegory of the cave where people saw truth in shadows and not what was the source of the shadows. I believe that, eventually, science will find that everything began with God. And, I believe science will eventually realize that God will be the end of scientific discovery. Pope Benedict XVI professed that science is "unable to grasp the global nature of reality" (December 22, 2005). My parents believed that God is reality. They believed that God is beyond our comprehension and that He is mysterious, but that He does exist. He who says God does not exist is lost, lifeless and already dead. If God exists, so does the Adversary - Satan. Scripture says so and so does Jesus. Who would dare say that the devil does not exist? As Charles Baudelaire wrote, "the finest trick of the devil is to persuade you that he does not exist." My parents recognized Jesus as the Christ of God and the Savior of humankind, but they did not subscribe to any one Christian denomination. We did not go to church on Sundays, but we did pray and study the Bible. Our Sundays were much like the Jewish Sabbath.

Like Jews, we left behind the stresses and confines of the world, so we could devote ourselves to God. It was a day of peace when God made us to lie down in green pastures, lead us beside still waters, restored our souls and lead us in paths of righteousness for His name's sake (Psalm 23). It was a day of rest, rejuvenation and prayer that we waited for each week. Our Sunday worship may not have been filled with ceremony and historical tradition, like the Jewish celebration of the Sabbath, but I believe our hearts were in the same place as practicing Jews. My parents were well versed in the

Bible and they felt the same natural piety to observe a holy day that honored God's rest at the end of Creation:

> And on the seventh day God finished his work which he had done, and he rested on the seventh day from all his work which he had done. So God blessed the seventh day and hallowed it, because on it God rested from all his work which he had done in creation (Genesis 2:2).

Music was important in our house and was not neglected on Sundays. Black American Gospel music helped us get closer to God because of the musicians' devotion to God's Son Jesus the Christ and the music's message of the Good News of God's Kingdom of Heaven. Gospel music's depth and power cannot be denied. Those singers and musicians were not merely entertainers, but brothers and sisters who we related to in heavenly ecstasy and worldly pain. Mahalia Jackson, Aretha Franklin and the Five Blind Boys of Mississippi kept us centered in this turbulent world and helped us get by during rough days.

My parents were everything to me, so when they died, my young innocent world crumbled.

I was twelve. It was a Friday night. The weather was beautiful and the stars were as bright as ever - perfect for a romantic evening. My parents decided to go out on a date just the two of them as a couple. Our neighbor was taking care of me. It was the end of the summer, the time of season when kids are preparing to go to college and are saying goodbye to their old friends. The college years is a time when most young adults are living independent of their parents for the first time, when they are on their own making their own decisions. It is a time when many blossom into maturity in front of the community. It is an exhilarating time when everything is new and they are learning about themselves. However, it can also be a reckless time when young adults feel indomitable as though there are no consequences to their actions - youth's greatest lie. Some fail life's lessons and reality confronts them when it is too late. My parents and I paid the price for one such youth's reckless behavior. She was drinking. She was underage. Her friend hosted a party at his parents' house. His parents did not promote the drinking, but neither did they stop it. The girl and a few friends decided to leave the party and get in her car to drive to their respective houses. She was supposed to be the sober designated driver, but she got carried away in pleasures of the party. She told the police that she only had a couple of drinks, but that was enough to dull her senses. My parents, too, were on their way home. Father was a cautious driver. He would tell me, "You have to be careful on the road because you never know who is doing what behind the wheel. When I step into my car, safety is top priority because not only could I injure myself, I could injure someone else and I would have to live with that for the rest of my life." The girl who was driving was not paying attention to the road. Her friends were joking around in the backseat of her car and she turned around to see why they were laughing. She hit my parents' car from the back. It swerved to the right, then to the left into oncoming traffic. A massive truck was driving toward them and hit them head on. Their car was destroyed and they died instantly. They were the only casualties. It was on the local television news. It was horrific. As an adult, I looked for answers and learned details. When I lost them, I was a child. They, too, were young. Both were thirty-four.

I used to blame the parents who allowed the underage drinking and the reckless college girl for my parents' deaths, but then I stopped because blame will not heal my sickness - my parents are gone and nothing can bring them back. In anger and frustration, I used to ask myself, "Why do good people suffer misfortune? Where is God when there is pain?" In Scripture, there is a parable about how God gave the homeless Lazarus - whose sores were licked by stray dogs - relief and eternal peace after death in Paradise. I believe God is good and just and that righteousness will prevail, even if it must be after death. As I dig deep, I hear Jesus cry out to me and to those suffering in this life in this world, "I know your pain!" because he took the form of a human being in flesh and experienced the peak of human suffering by being nailed to a cross for hours and left to die - a torture reserved for criminals, not something we would imagine for the Sinless One. And, to those who have lost loved ones in their lives, to parents who have lost their children (perhaps, life's greatest ill), God cries out to them, "I know your pain!" because His only Son was tortured and killed. Understanding this about Jesus the Christ and God the Father, I find comfort because I know I am not alone. If God and His Son experienced pain, we are not immune to it either.

I believe God never leaves us, even when we think He has. This sentiment is illustrated in mother's favorite poem, *Footprints in the Sand.* In it, a man has a dream about his life with God of which is represented by two sets of footprints on a beach. He notices that during his most difficult times, there is only one set and so questions God's presence. The poem ends with God comforting and reassuring the man that when he saw only one set of footprints on the beach, it was not that God was not by his side, but rather that God was carrying him. This poem hung framed on father and mother's bedroom wall. They often referred to it in conversation and they pointed it out to me more than once. As a child, its imagery left an impression on me and now as an adult, I consider it angelic. When I am troubled and in distress, I go to it and it strengthens me and reminds me of mother. It helped her and it has helped me. Even after death, father and mother still teach me about life and love.

They helped shaped my character and helped direct me to God intentionally and unintentionally, in specific ways and in implicit influences. God was the center of their universe and by means of His Grace and Love, He made that possible. God strengthened them and He has strengthened me and He is the center of my universe, as well.

I miss my parents, but their love for me lives in me and is a part of me coming through with every action I take. I sometimes think about the mystery and power of love. In English, we use the word "love" in many ways. We say we love art, our pets and God with the same word. The ancient Greeks tried to capture, pinpoint and distinguish the many forms of love with four words: storge, philia, eros, agape.

Many years after my parents' deaths, I had a desire to understand the meaning of love. It helped me cope with my loss. By studying it, my feelings for them were no longer undefinable. I know they loved me and I know they knew I loved them, but I had an ethereal understanding of our relationship. Studying about love was therapeutic and helped me make sense of our love. I was able to extract its meaning through study.

The ancient Greeks used the term "storge" to describe a fondness, affection and love that holds a family together. My parents' love for me and my love for them is the epitome of storge. My mother squeezing me as a child for no other reason than because she loved me is storge in its purest form. She demonstrated her storge for me when she would labor in the kitchen to make me homemade angel hair pasta with sauce made fresh from the tomatoes in our garden because it was my favorite meal. I have had spaghetti and tomato sauce in restaurants, but it does not compare to my mother's cooking. I felt my parents' storge for me when they would give me butterfly kisses on Saturday mornings and when they would read a story to me at night and then tuck me into bed. I tried to reciprocate their storge for me with hand crafted birthday cards that said things like, "World's Best Father" and "World's Best Mother." Storge is a comfortable, quiet, private feeling that I smelled in mother's perfume and in father's aftershave. It comes to me when I see yellow lilies like the ones that were in front of our home. I found it in father's jokes and in mother's laugh. Father had a dry wit that mother appreciated. He was a master of puns and would play with words. One of father's regular jokes was, "You can tune a guitar, but you can't _tuna_ fish. Unless of course, you play _bass_" (Douglas Adams). Mother must have heard that joke a thousand times, but she always laughed, as if to say, "That's my husband, at it again, and I love him."

Storge extends beyond parent and child to connect all family members, humanity and even animals. As 20th century British author, academic and lay theologian C.S. Lewis explains in _The Four Loves_, storge "ignores the barriers of age, sex, class and education. It can exist between a clever young man from the university and an old nurse, though their minds inhabit different worlds" (Lewis, *The Four Loves*, Harcourt Inc, 32). Storge can be a love shared between a man and his dog. A dog has storge for her newborn puppies and a cat has storge for her newborn kittens. Sometimes, even a dog and a cat can have storge for each other.

YOUNG EZEKIEL
A LIFE OF LOVES

TWO

PHILIA

My parents and I shared a small world inhabited by only the three of us. I never saw any relatives and though my parents had many acquaintances, they had few friends. These things did not matter to them because our small world was filled with storge. We thought that all we needed was each other and our storge. It was a beautiful world that one day was no more.

After my parents' deaths, my future was uncertain and I was vulnerable to the outside world. But, I was lucky. My grandmother's sister - an aunt who I never met - rescued me from the lost life that seemed to be ahead of me. My mother never mentioned her. In fact, my parents never spoke about family because both felt their families were highly dysfunctional. Father never met his father because my grandfather left my grandmother while my grandmother was pregnant with father. My grandfather was a gambler and could not support his wife and son, so he left them. He was a con-man who preyed on women and would take their money and when he had his fill, he would abandon them. My father's mother was irresponsible, as well. She neglected father during his youth. She inherited a family estate with a great sum of money and was very intelligent and made sure father went to school, but she used drugs and failed to care for father. Father pretty much raised himself. My grandmother never fully recovered from her addictions and was in and out of rehabilitation centers for most of her life. I remember father calling my mother his angel because he believed she saved him from his dark life. Mother had great sympathy and compassion for father. He was smart and strong and overcame his hard life and mother fell in love with him because of this. Mother's family was also troubled and it was money that tore them apart. When my grandfather died prematurely from a heart attack, my grandmother manipulated his will to acquire mother's inheritance. My grandmother said she did so because she was sick with cancer and needed to pay for treatment. The judge sided with my grandmother, but mother was convinced that my grandmother stole her inheritance to sustain her affluent lifestyle. I learned all this from my grandmother's sister, my Aunt Gerontissa, when I was old enough to inquire and understand. My aunt was level headed and gave me her more objective perspective. My aunt told me money tears families apart too often. Money is powerful and can pervert one's character. If one cannot forgive, relationships are doomed. My parents were born and raised near Boston, but moved to Omorfi to start a new life.

My aunt stayed in Massachusetts. When she learned about my parents' deaths, she brought me back. My aunt was not a native of the United States. She was an immigrant born in the homeland and was a child during World War II. She was fifteen when the war ended and grew up in the aftermath when the nations were trying to recover from the devastation. In those formative years, she acquired much of her knowledge about the world and the individual on her own and she matured quickly on the streets. She was street smart. From her life experiences, she gathered information and saw patterns of when people prevailed and lost that helped her to make better decisions. She observed the piety of the priest, the erudition of the scholar, the lasciviousness of the whore and the greed of the miser. No one is perfect and she noticed when the priest was lazy and when the scholar was foolish and she observed redemption in the whore's honesty and the miser's frugality. She applied what she learned to her own life, which made her wise. As I got to know her, Aunt Gerontissa knew what was inside of people because she was keenly aware of herself and to know oneself is to know what is inside others. As Socrates learned from the oracle of Delphi, "Know thyself." To know thyself is to know what dwells inside the individual and to know the human condition. She believed that we are all the same - we are all human beings all living on the same planet. We all experience love and pain and we can all relate to each other's joy and sorrow. She was sensitive to her own feelings and the feelings of others which gave her compassion. To know thyself is easier said than done. It could take a lifetime, but if one perseveres, one will notice treasures multiplying within.

My aunt was a stout and physically strong woman. She reminded me of a bull; not because she had a short temper, but because she had a powerful presence. She demanded respect, but was never rude. She rarely laughed; although, her kindness often shined through her serious disposition. Her hair was short, grey and wavy. Some women dye their hair, but my aunt never got carried away with looks. She had seen so much during her life that looks were of little importance. In the house, she wore robes and slippers that matched. Most of her robes were shades of purple, her favorite color. Outside the house, she wore dark colored blouses and dresses. The weight of the clothing depended on the outside temperature. A seamstress by trade, she worked in a shop, but also in her home for family and friends. She was frugal and wise with money. If a customer had disposable fabric that he or she did not want, my aunt would make a bag, scarf or hat out of it and sell it in the shop she worked in. She was clever and her creations were ingenious. Outside her kitchen door she kept a large clay pot to put banana peels, apple cores and the like as compost. She would use the compost to fertilize her vegetable garden and rose bushes. When my aunt was not working, she was usually tending to her gardens. People around town knew her as the women with the beautiful rose bushes. They grew in her front lawn where people walking and driving by could see and admire them. In the backyard, she grew her vegetable garden, which took up half of the space. It was Edenesque. Cucumbers, eggplants and tomatoes flourished during the warm seasons. She had a pear tree and grape vines, which grew along her wooden fence. She even had a fig tree that in the summer produced the best figs on the east coast. She liked being outside. She did not have a television or computer - things that usually keep people indoors. She rose with the sun and set with the sun. When she was cooking, she had the hands of a magician. But, she never kept secrets. If her neighbor asked her how she put together her chicken cutlet with mushroom sauce, she proudly passed on the recipe. Many people tried to cook her meals, but no one could compare. She was a master chef.

After my parents' deaths, I was angry with God. But, my aunt was very religious and because of her influence on me during those formative years, my anger did not last long. When I was a child, my parents taught me about God and Jesus the Christ, but they did not follow an organized formal Christianity. We never attended Sunday services, but I never missed a Sunday service with my aunt.

About once a month, my aunt and I visited the nuns at the nunnery. It took about an hour and a half to get there, but it was all highway. It was the furthest my aunt would drive in her car. It was not because the car could not handle it; but because my aunt, at her age, did not have the same stamina to drive as she used to. At the nunnery, we would help the nuns with chores which gave us the opportunity to talk to them and learn from them. Being in their presence was enough to edify. They always wore black, but they were filled with joy because of their relationship with God and Jesus. It was not an easy life. They had to endure the ascetical struggle to purify themselves for the Lord. However, if you asked them, they would tell you there is no other life to live. None of them would leave. Their devotion to God and Jesus was too strong. Annually, my aunt and I would buy from the nuns a homemade vasilopita to celebrate the new year. It was a round sweet bread that had inside it a coin, which would bring the recipient good luck for the year. We also visited to buy icons, books and recorded chanting - not always for us, but also as gifts for loved ones. My aunt's devotion to the Church compelled her to fast. Throughout the year, she would fast from meat and dairy on Wednesdays and Fridays. The Church selected those days to mourn when Jesus was betrayed by Judas and when he suffered on the Cross. Plus, for over forty days during Great Lent, she would fast to prepare for Easter. She would cook, so I adopted her fasting lifestyle.

My relationship with the Church reached a new phase when I was an adolescent; I was skeptical about the Bible and the Church. I thought that because the Bible was written by man, it was not perfect and filled with error. I now reflect on this and it is an understandable objection, but at the time I did not understand the power of the Holy Spirit and how it guides man and moves him to write about God in the Light of God. I believed that the Church, too, was filled with error, but unlearned, I did not understand that the Church Fathers created the Church to preserve the authenticity of the faith. Yes, man created it, but a body was necessary, so the belief and teachings of Christ could continue to guide and teach man here on earth until Christ returns. Though my connection to the Church was weak, during this time in my life, I always knew that God existed. I thought to myself, how could we be so vain to think that we know everything and deny God?

As I was growing up, I had a problem with money and thought money caused people to do wicked things. My family history shaped my perspective and I believe my conclusions were justifiable. However, my aunt explained to me that money does not have to be evil. In fact, it could be valuable and used to do good works. My aunt opened my eyes and showed me a different perspective. She was a member of the Greek Ladies Philoptochos

Society. Philoptochos is a Greek word that means "friend of the poor." It is one of the largest women's philanthropic organization in the United States. The women are known as the mothers of a Greek Orthodox Christian children's home called Saint Basil Academy in Garrison, NY. The children of Saint Basil Academy have troubled backgrounds, like my own, but do not have an aunt, like mine, to adopt them. I thank God every day that my aunt took me in. She did not have to, but her storge for me compelled her. Saint Basil Academy provides a refuge for children whose parents or guardians are unable to care for them due to illness, death, chemical addiction and other problems. Through the guiding light of the Greek Orthodox Christian Church, it provides a nurturing environment where they are strengthened by a support system that allows them to flourish and become meaningful members of society. It provides a beacon of hope and a safe haven for them by ensuring material, spiritual, and emotional support for the development of the whole person: body, mind, and spirit. The staff of Saint Basil Academy provides the structure that they need through hours of selfless giving. Through the behavior modification program, the children are taught accountability and responsibility for themselves. The Director of Saint Basil Academy is Father Costa, a powerful, yet gentle shepherd who leads his flock with love. Saint Basil Academy's mission is to teach, to heal, to bring the light of Christ to young lives. (Saint Basil Academy on-line brochure). My aunt explained to me that money can be a blessing from God and it could be used to fulfill God's will. She told me about Saint John Chrysostom. Born around 350 AD, John was given the name "Chrysostom," which in Greek means "Golden Mouth," because of the sublimity of his preaching. In *On Wealth and Poverty*, John, filled with the Holy Spirit, gives his transcendent view of money. He explains that those who have money are blessed with it by God and to not share one's possessions is theft. God has given the wealthy their money, but it also belongs to the poor:

> He [the rich man] is directed to distribute it to his fellow servants who are in want. So if he spends more on himself than his need requires, he will pay the harshest penalty in the hereafter. For his own goods are not his own, but belong to his fellow servants (John Chrysostom, *On Wealth and Poverty*, SVS Press, 50).

I believe those who give to the children of Saint Basil Academy give from their hearts. They may not need to hear John's theology, but they can find reassurance in his words that what they are doing is divine.

Every Sunday, I went to church services with my aunt. I remember how impressed I was with the icons in the church, particularly the one of Christ Pantocrator - Christ the Almighty. It is the icon of

Christ blessing His people as ruler of all Creation and it is located at the dome of every Greek Orthodox Christian Church. The church is filled with icons and each one is magnificent. The artist's careful attention to detail in creating such an intricate image is awe-inspiring. It is mystifying how the artist can create these massive images with such fine precision, particularly mystifying are those that are mosaics, which are made of tiny stones. As a child, I knew Christ was the Son of God, but I also knew that he was a man and I was always puzzled at why the Orthodox icons did not look realistic. The Orthodox icons are not like photographs. They are in Byzantine style and represent an ideal image, inner spiritual nature and other-worldly quality of the subject. They glorify God, His Son, Mother Mary, the martyrs and the saints. Historically, the icons were meant to help the laity to connect with God and teach them lessons and theology the Church believes are of supreme importance. As a child, they left me captivated and wondering. Closest to my heart were the icons of children martyrs that adorn the walls inside the chapel. These children, who were as young as I was when I was first struck by their images, died because they stood up to persecution and would not deny their love for Christ. They were filled with great strength and I desired to be as strong as them. 2nd century Church theologian Tertullian famously said that "the blood of the martyrs is the seed of the Church." The martyrs' bloody deaths and their strength to not deny their love for Christ propagated the faith. I can envision onlookers puzzled by a Christian martyr's death ask one another, "Who are these people who face death without fear and what do they believe in?" The answer that traveled the land was that they are Christians and they believe in Jesus the Christ. The children whose images adorn the chapel walls were filled with courage and they gave me courage.

Most Sundays, I did not want to go to church, but when the services were over, I felt the Holy Spirit in me. Sometimes, on my way home, I would sing and hum the hymns. I did not realize it, but the Christianity in me was growing. It affected me.

Every season in Massachusetts gave me a different taste of God's Glorious Creation. In the autumn, the colorful leaves brightened the horizon. In the winter, the white snow descending from the sky aroused in me the spirit of Christmas. In the spring, the earth and all that inhabit it came alive in anticipation of Easter. In the summer, the radiant sun warmed me and magnified the sky. Year-round the grounds were bursting with beauty. It was much different than Omorfi and the beaches I knew so well.

My aunt's home was a single story ranch-style house. The surface of the exterior was made of cream-colored stucco. Most of the houses in the neighborhood were ranch-style, as well. They were all built in the 1950s when the architectural design was at its peak of popularity. Other exterior facades included brick, stone and wood. Trees separated the houses. In front of many of the houses, beyond their lawns, were short free dry-stone walls that bordered the roads and peeking out of each entrance stood mailboxes. People jogged along roads and bicyclists pedaled along with them. Cars would wiz by them, but the joggers and bicyclists did not care. Nothing distracted them from their sports. Surrounding my new home was nature. Trees were everywhere and little animals rustled in the leaves and birds chirped in the air. I often saw deer scamper in the forests. Calm and quiet, I would try to get close to them and I always felt special to witness their graceful honesty.

One late summer day, a couple of weeks after I moved into my new home, I was in the public park on the basketball court shooting jump-shots by myself. I was there for about twenty minutes when a group of boys, all about my age, gathered together on the other side of the court. I kept on shooting and after each shot, I glanced over to see what they were doing. One of the boys was tying his shoe. Another one was drinking from his water bottle. The remaining boys were playing on the court. They were all joking around and laughing. I kept to myself even though it looked like they were having fun. Then, from the corner of my eye, I noticed that one of the boys was walking in my direction, but I pretended that I did not see him. As he approached me, he called out, "Hey buddy." I was a bit stunned and said, "How's it going?" Then, he said, "My friends and I want to start a game, but we are short one person. Do you want to play?" I quickly said, "Definitely." Then, he said, "Cool." As I picked up my ball and my stuff that lay on the ground, he took a step closer and introduced himself. "I'm Mike," he said. "I'm Ezekiel," I said. "I never heard that name before," he said. "Yeah, I know. It's a little weird," I said. "No. I think it's cool," he said. Then, we walked over to the other boys and Mike said, "I found a player. His name is Ezekiel." They each gave me a big smile. By the time the game was over, I felt like I was a part of their crew. Mike and the boys were my first friends in my new home.

Mike's best friend was Gabe and soon, Gabe became my good friend, too. Mike, Gabe and I were inseparable. The three of us were the same age, lived in the same neighborhood and went to the same school. We hung out with other children, but - autumn, winter, spring and summer - we were always together. We did the same things most boys did, but we did them together. We spent a lot of time in the wooded trails that were practically in our backyards. Hundreds of acres of nature were preserved for hiking enthusiasts, wildlife watchers and young explorers and adventurers, like us. We trekked through the trails often and knew the nooks and crannies around every turn. We had our favorite spots and usually gravitated to the waters. There were places where bold brooks fell from high rocks, pounding and pulsating on the stalwart rocks below. In the meandering streams, salamanders slipped and slid through the moss-covered rock faces. Creeks crept around rough rocky corners. And, in the still ponds on the floating lily pads, frogs ribbited and toads croaked. Sometimes, we went fishing and other times, we went swimming. These images remain steadfast in my memory. My love for Mike and Gabe is deep because their friendships helped me recover from my parents' deaths. They were there for me when I needed them most, even if they did not know it. They did not hesitate to love me as their friend. The ancient Greeks called this love between friends "philia." The 4th century BC Greek philosopher Aristotle was one of the first to analyze philia's nuances. In his work *Nicomachean Ethics*, he devotes sections (or books) 8 and 9 to exploring its meaning and its relevance in our lives.

C.S. Lewis calls philia the least natural love because we can survive without it. Eros (romantic love) begets us, storge (familial love) rears us, agape (Christian love) brings us closer to our Maker, but we can probably live without philia (friendship love). Friends are not obligated to be friends. Mike and Gabe did not have to talk to me at the basketball court. They could have ignored me. I had nothing to offer them, but they welcomed me into their group and I am happy that they did. We chose to be friends. Philia is not bound or confined by natural tendencies the way storge and eros are. Philia is a free love. It is a spiritual love that raises us almost above humanity. "It is the sort of love one can imagine between angels" (Lewis, *The Four Loves*, Harcourt Inc, 77). We do not need friends, yet they enrich our lives. In ancient times, philia was exalted because it is something we all want. As Aristotle points out, "No one would choose to live without friends, even if he had all other goods" (Aristotle, *Nicomachean Ethics*, The Library of Liberal Arts, 214). Even if I was the richest man in the world, I would still want friends. One might say they are "the greatest of external goods" (Aristotle, 263). I felt honored to be Mike and Gabe's friend. Who would not be honored to be chosen to be a friend? They express their philia for me and I reciprocate with my philia for them. This mutual love is praiseworthy and is the sign of a true lasting friendship. Mike and Gabe have integrity and are honest, sincere and true to themselves and because they have these qualities within themselves, they are like that with me, too. We did our best to not lower ourselves below these virtues and we never steered one another toward base activities. In fact, we prevent each other from making base decisions. "What characterizes good men is that they neither go wrong themselves nor let their friends do so" (Aristotle, 230). Furthermore, as 6th century BC Greek lyrical poet Theognis said, "You will learn noble things from noble people" (Aristotle, 265).

There was one time, when Mike, Gabe and I trekked through the woods to the waterfall. It was about a fifteen minute walk from our homes and as one approaches the waterfall, there is a heavy stream running from it. We usually went during the summer and would swim in the shallow pool below the falling water. It is an extraordinary sight. The waterfall is about three stories tall. Each time I went, I was awed. However, the water was cold; nothing like the water at Omorfi, but I would go in anyway. This one time, when we arrived, a group of kids were splashing and fooling around. Mike, Gabe and I stationed ourselves on a giant slab of rock under a tree beside the pool and then we inched our way into the water. We walked over to the falling water and let it beat on our backs. It was the best massage. We mixed into the other group to be friendly, but a couple of guys were standoffish though the girls were nice to us. As I started to talk to one of the girls, one of the guys bumped into me on purpose. He gave me a tough look and said, "Watch your step." I was caught off guard and replied with, "Excuse me." Then, he asked, "What's your name?" I answered, "Ezekiel." "Well, Ezekiel," he said, "I dare you to jump from the waterfall." I was young, fourteen years old, and froze. Mike was big for a fourteen year old and was the star center for the high school junior varsity basketball team. As the guy was pestering me, Mike stepped in and said, "Why are you daring my friend?" The guy said, "I think your friend is afraid" and then he started laughing and looking at his friends. Mike said, "What are you trying to do, impress your friends by making my friend look foolish? It doesn't take much to pick on someone smaller than you." When he confronted the guy, the guy said, "I was just trying to be funny." Mike asked, "Have you ever jumped off this cliff?" "No," the guy answered. "Then how can you dare my friend, if you have never jumped?" Mike asked. At first, when the guy bumped into me, he used his size to intimidate me and was swelling with pride, but when Mike stepped in, his ego deflated and he shrunk in size. After that, they respected Mike and me, too, because I was with Mike. Mike kept it real. He told it like it was and spoke to him with respect. Their cold front warmed and, believe it or not, we all ended up becoming friends.

Aristotle explains that bad people never have true long lasting friendships because they lack integrity and are not constant with themselves and therefore cannot be constant with others. Bad people "do not find joy in one another, unless they see some material advantage coming to them" (Aristotle, 222). Bad people do not have true friendships.

Aristotle explains that there are three forms of philia: love for those who are useful, pleasant and good. There are different motives in each form of philia. For example, philia based on usefulness is concerned with the good gained by the other. The relationships between an employer and employee or a teacher and student are examples of philia based on usefulness. Each party sustains the friendship as long as the usefulness for one another lasts. When one thinks he is getting less than he should, there are bound to be complaints and reproaches. Philia based on pleasure, too, only last as long as each party maintains that sense of pleasure. One who finds pleasure in a funny person feels philia for him up until the pleasure ends. But, here, complaints and reproaches do not usually arise because the two parties will simply no longer spend time together. Philia based on usefulness and pleasure are not based on the type of person one is, but because of what is gained. As a result, friendships such as these easily dissolve. Aristotle suggests that when a friendship ends, one should not treat the friend as a stranger, but rather remember that he was once a friend. We should treat him better than a stranger, unless it was his wickedness that ended the friendship (Aristotle, 252). Mike and Gabe are more than friends of utility and pleasure - though they are useful and pleasant because they are good people. They are my good friends. There are many people who I like and get along with and think are good people, but Mike and Gabe are my truest friends. It is impossible to be perfect friends with many people. Like romantic love, it is "an extreme, and an extreme tends to be unique" (Aristotle, 225). Mike and Gabe always looked out for me. They wanted the best for me and I knew it and they knew I would be there for them. When I was down they picked me up. Those "who wish for their friends' good for their friends' sake are friends of the truest sense" (Aristotle, 219). People who share common interests will be companions, but those who share something more will be friends. Friends share something "more inward, less widely shared and less easily defined" (Lewis, 66). They walk side by side seeking a common truth, sharing a common vision. A person should neither have no friends nor too many. Perhaps, the largest number of true friends is limited to the number one might be able to live with (Aristotle, 268). In true friendships, quality is important, not quantity. In true friendships, just as it is in friendships of pleasure, "a few friends are sufficient, just as it takes little to give food the right amount of sweetness" (Aristotle, 267). Mike, Gabe and I grew up together. From the time I moved to Massachusetts at the age of twelve, I have few memories without them. We were constantly in and out of each other's houses and even our families were close. In our friendship, we were equals. There was no leader in our crew and there were no followers. We each had a voice and we respected each other's opinions. We joked with each other, but we never let our jokes go too far to the point of hurting each other. We knew each other's limits and only joked with each other out of philia.

Like everyone who has a friend, our relationships strengthened as we earned each other's confidence. It starts off small, like how Gabe let me review his class notes for a quiz. Or, how Mike let me borrow some money to buy a drink on our walk home from school. On my fourteenth birthday, they each gave me fourteen birthday punches. My arm was sore with bruises for nearly two weeks, but they did it out of philia because they were also the ones who were ready to back me up when I almost got into a fight with two boys on the basketball court outside of school. This was when I knew they were true friends. I trusted them and they trusted me. They never intentionally wronged me. People who become friends quickly without knowing each other's worth are not really friends even though they want to be. A true friendship takes time to grow.

We had other friends, for example, in class, on sports teams and in clubs. And, in that extended group, most of our friends were friends with each other. "One's friends should also be the friends of one another, if they are all going to spend their days in each other's company" (Aristotle, 268). There was a group of us that played sports. We were competitive and always tried to outdo each other, but it was always in good spirit. We were constantly racing each other to see who could run the fastest. It made us better athletes and because we were friends, we never let the competition get the best of us. I was athletic and strong with good stamina. I was good at sports, better than most, but not exceptional at any one sport. Autumn, winter, spring, summer - we played whatever sport was in season. We played in the town's recreation leagues, but we mostly played amongst each other. Our town had baseball, football and soccer fields; plus, basketball and tennis courts. After homework, we would call each other and get a ball and play until the sun set. The weekends were more of the same. Weather often dictated the chosen sport. Football during the first snowfall became an annual tradition. Snow often accumulated from inches into feet and all us friends were of the consensus that the more the better. We would bundle up in layers of clothing to protect ourselves from nature's elements, but by the end, the jackets and gloves would come off. We took it serious enough that we would sweat in the snow to the point of being soaked inside and out. However, by the end, rules were relinquished and rabblerousing and fooling around reigned. We would often pounce on each other even without possession of the ball just to fall in the soft forgiving snow. Frozen fingers and drenched threads were normal, but it was always a day well spent. For Mike, Gabe and I, our favorite sport, by far, was basketball. We would play all-year-round: outside on black-tops and inside the town's youth center gymnasium. We each had our own style of play, but we also tried to imitate the moves of our favorite players. Our hero was Michael Jordan - perhaps, the greatest athlete of the 20th century. He was the best at offense and defense, a complete player who lead his team to six championships. He injected creativity and artistry into his play on the court. He played at the highest level in every game because he believed every game was important. He wanted to prove that he was the best and he did while mesmerizing, delighting and awing the crowd (including many of his opponents). He made it look easy, but that is because he sharpened his skills with hard practice. When he failed, he practiced harder and it motivated him to be better. God made him tall and strong and blessed him with a tenacity beyond all other athletes, but he seized those gifts and with a profound work ethic, he made himself the best. In one of his most lauded games, he played sick with the flu and a 103 degree fever and through his indomitable will, he scored 38 points leading his team to victory.

We loved music, too, and the music of Bob Marley was especially meaningful to us. Marley's music is everywhere: radio, television, parties, movies, friends. It is a part of our culture. By the time I was fifteen, I was already numb to his songs. But, one day, Mike, Gabe and I were in Gabe's house lounging on the couches in his living room, hanging out and passing time. Gabe left for a moment and went to his bedroom. When he returned to us, he said, "Fellas, I've got something you've got to hear." "What's that?" I asked. "Bob Marley," he said with a grin on his face. "What's with the excitement? We know it all," Mike said. "Not this stuff," Gabe said proudly. Gabe hooked up the music to the speakers. We got quite and then the music kicked in. It had a heavy rhythm and then we heard Marley's voice: "I'm a rebel, soul rebel. I'm a capturer, soul adventurer." I liked it. I thought it had value, but after the song ended, I did not think much of it. The following Thursday was the anniversary of my parents' deaths. I was hurting. I was sitting on the stoop of my aunt's house and Gabe passed by and saw me. He asked me if I was alright, which meant a lot because he cared. I told him why I was upset. The next day when the three of us were walking together to school, I was still visibly down. Gabe handed me some music and said, "I've got something that may help out." It was an album of some of Bob Marley's early recordings with songs I never heard before. When I returned home and listened to the album, I noticed that the rhythms were uplifting and the lyrics were spiritual. Much of his music hit home. It was like medicine to my sick soul. I was hooked when I heard the song, "I'm Hurting Inside" because I, too, hurt inside. We were coming from the same place, so when Marley sang, "One Love! One Heart! Let's get together and feel all right," I knew things would get better. He preached love, peace, unity, freedom and Jah (God). In songs such as "Thank You Lord," he proclaimed how he loved to pray. Songs like "Exodus" are powerful and helped me make it through tough times. He was not a saint. He was notorious for smoking marijuana and having affairs with women; even so, most of his music is angelic. The youth are impressionable and Marley's indiscretions may seem cool, but my friends and I did not admire him for the marijuana and women; we thought he was cool because of his music.

We value our friends in bad fortune and in good fortune. They are indispensable in bad fortune because we need their assistance. In sorrow, they can alleviate our pain by sharing our burden or by the pleasantness of their presence. If a friend is tactful, "seeing him and talking to him are a source of comfort, since he knows our character and the things which give us pleasure or pain" (Aristotle, 270). They are a refuge during times of misfortune. I do not know how I would have made it through the trauma of my parents' deaths without the Mike and Gabe. We need them in good fortune, too, because it is the best way to live. They give us the opportunity to share our joy. When I finally passed my test at the Department of Motor Vehicles and got my driver's license, I could barely wait to tell Mike and Gabe. I was excited and feeling their joy for me was just as meaningful as getting the license.

The opinions of my friends, "of this little circle, while I am in it, outweighs that of a thousand outsiders... Theirs is the praise we really covet and the blame we really dread" (Lewis, 79). Lewis illustrates that a group of friends have the power to stir rebellion. With a common vision, they can change the establishment for better or worse. He explains that "the dangers are perfectly real. Friendship (as the ancients [like Aristotle] saw) can be a school of virtue; but also (as they did not see) a school of vice. It is ambivalent. It makes good men better and bad men worse" (Lewis, 80). After Jesus tells his disciples to love one another as he has loved them, he calls them friends and together they changed the world.

I was able to love Mike and Gabe because I loved myself first. A "man is his own best friend and therefore should have the greatest affection for himself" (Aristotle, 260). This may sound selfish, but if a man does not love himself, how can he love another? How would he know what love is? My love for them was an extension of the love I had for myself. A person who acts justly to himself, who acts with self-control, who seeks to be virtuous cannot be called selfish. He desires what is noble, not what is advantageous. A good man's noble deeds benefit himself because he fulfills his desire to be noble and the recipient of those noble deeds benefits, as well, so both parties win. A wicked man's selfish deeds may fulfill his desire, but he fails to feed the greatest that is in him: love, nobility, virtue. If he chooses to not do what is best for himself, he will not do what is best for another. I believe by loving yourself, by doing what is best for yourself, you will make a true friend.

A person does not need to know every detail of another's life to be a friend. As Lewis writes, "the real question [is], *Do you see the same truth?* In a circle of true friends each man is simply what he is: stands for nothing but himself" (Lewis, 70). I did not need to know that Mike had an older sister who was married with kids or that Gabe liked to read books to be my friend. And, they did not ask to know about my past, so I could qualify to be their friend. Of course, we learned these things as we spent more time together during comments, jokes and stories we told one another, but never as questions to pass a test. My friendships with them began neutral with no proof of who we were and no direction, but when our honest selves came out and because we saw the same truth, then we were able to walk side by side as perfect friends. The more I got to know them and the more I experienced with them, the more I appreciated them. Our philia for each other was so great that each of us felt lucky to have the others. Deep inside, I would ask myself, "Who am I to be blessed with such friends?" It was very humbling. We were free to say and do as we pleased without fear of being judged because we knew each other so well - nothing one could say or do would be a surprise to the rest. When the three of us were together, we brought out the best in each other. We talked philosophy before we were aware of philosophy as an enterprise. We talked about our ambitions and girls. We talked with comfort, ease and joy. The richest moments were those when the air was thick with laughter. We would often laugh for no reason other than because we enjoyed each other's company. Lewis calls times like these "the golden sessions" and that "Life - natural life - has no better gift to give" (Lewis, 72). We knew friendships like ours were rare and I remember saying to myself and to them that these are the best moments of our lives.

There is a movie that Mike, Gabe and I enjoyed called *Stand by Me*. It is a story about four young boys, friends who journey together through prairies and forests to find a dead body, one they learned about in their hometown. The substance of the story is the boys' relationships and their loss of innocence. At the end of the story, one of the boys who was now a man, a writer, reflects on this experience and says, "I never had any friends later on like the ones I had when I was twelve. Jesus, does anyone?" This sentiment was shared between me and my friends and is an insight that has remained with me throughout life.

One of my favorite childhood memories took place outside Gabe's house. There were four of us: myself, Mike, Gabe and our friend Alex. It was a beautiful summer day and the breeze in the air alleviated much of the sun's heat. It was after lunch, but before dinner. At that age, playtime revolved around breakfast, lunch and dinner because my aunt and their mothers wanted to make sure we did not miss a meal. It was a little past mid-summer when the excitement of summer started to subside. We were bored and spent a good half of an hour tossing a football around. Mike interrupted the rhythm and threw the football at the backboard of the basketball rim that was set up in Gabe's driveway. A new game began. We all took turns trying to throw the football at the backboard and after each successful throw, we increased the distance between us and the backboard.

However, this, too, got boring. Our attention spans were sizzling. Gabe's parents were not home, which was an added ingredient to spice up our mischievous dispositions. Mayhem was inevitable. Gabe had a bunch of plum trees on his property, so instead of throwing the football, we decided to throw the fallen plums at each other. I don't know who fired the first shot, but we all picked up ammunition and aimed it at one another. The weapon was chosen. I got hit once and the plum juice stained my shirt and I was upset, but then I hit Mike, which was gratifying. Soon, we realized we had to set parameters and rules to our game; otherwise, it would be chaos and a disorganized game never lasts long because someone always gets hurt. We incorporated bases and timeouts; however, there was no objective to our game and no points or penalties. It was just an excellent idea. I asked myself, "Why did we not think of this before?" We split up into two teams. It was Mike and Gabe versus Alex and me. On his property, Gabe had a car garage that was separate from his house. The garage was one story tall, as was part of his house. Between these two buildings - these fortifications - were the driveway and a vegetable garden. It was brave to run though the driveway because we would be exposed, but we could quickly escape. The vegetable garden was a good place to hide, but it was difficult to run through. And, on the roofs, our only protection was prayer. The space was small enough where we could reach each other from one edifice to the other, yet large enough to make the game challenging. It was an ideal combat zone. We decided to climb onto the roofs and commence battle. Courage and confidence were clutch to conquering and claiming conquest. I think a lot of people would have freaked out being up so high, but not us. We were comfortable running on the roofs, jumping up and down one story buildings and dodging small inanimate objects aimed at each other because we were athletes with good balance. There were many trees and countless plums. Our arsenal was limited to plums, but we exploited our resources by the tactics we used. We hurled some of the plums into the air as grenades, released others with rapid fire and spread handfuls of others with a single throw. My principal strategy was to attack then immediately defend. I often employed a blitzkrieg, but then required a short reprieve to muster my military might and gather arms. Mike was always on the move and employed a moving target theory, which made him difficult to track and attack. Alex stationed himself under one of the trees which supplied unlimited ammo and he used a shovel he found in the open garage as a shield to protect himself. Gabe was less strategic and consequently slipped a few times on the mushed fruit. Fortunately, he was on the ground and not on one of the roofs. We probably would have been there until someone broke a bone, but a police officer heard us and saw us from a distance and commanded us to come down from the roofs -

disrupting our fun. At the end, we sat on the war torn landscape and the plum remains and juices that saturated the sun scolded cement and roofs, which emitted a unique mist and fruity smell. There was no victory claimed and no spoils won - other than a good time. As an adult looking back at my youthful years, I have scenes in my mind that emerge from my memory, but there are only a few events that are always with me which I will never forget. The plum battle is one of them.

I know I said philia is a freely chosen love, that we pick our friends, that we select those whom we might connect with. But, sometimes, I think something more transcendent, mystical and divine takes place. Life seems to be very delicate and complex. The slightest change can change the outcome of the following events. Everything has consequences. It is the principle of cause and effect. There are an infinite number of ways of how my parents could still be alive. And, there are an infinite number of ways of how I would not have met Mike and Gabe. If you asked me before my parents' deaths what my life would be like in the future, I never would have guessed the reality. Mike and Gabe are like family and I believe this is not by chance. C.S. Lewis said it best: "for a Christian, there are, strictly speaking, no chances. A secret Master of the Ceremonies has been at work. Christ, who said to the disciples 'Ye have not chosen me, but I have chosen you,' can truly say to every group of Christian friends

'You have not chosen one another but I have chosen you for one another'" (Lewis, 89).

For me, living with my aunt was a blessing on many levels. Geographically, it made a difference. As a child, the last thing I wanted to do was to leave Omorfi. It was my home and all I knew. But, looking back at my situation, I was better off moving away from Omorfi . Living in Massachusetts separated me from my parents' car accident. It alleviated the situation. It was the case of out of sight, out of mind. The physical distance between Omorfi and Massachusetts provided for me an emotional distance. And, the stark contrast between one another's landscape gave me a new start.

I revisited Omorfi when I was an adult, when I felt I was prepared to deal with the trauma, strong enough deal with the pain. As an adult whose wounds had managed to heal with a scar, I visited the roads and paths I traveled along as a child. They caused scenes of my life to flash before my eyes reminding me of my parents. The smell of the salt water, the feel of the rough sand sifting through my toes, the sound of children laughing and splashing water, the taste of the fresh fruit and the sight of my old house ignited a love in me that I missed. It was like a lucid dream that receded to the back of my mind that was reawakened. I cried when I revisited for the first time, but it was a good cry. During that first visit as a mature man, I felt as though my parents were with me, once again. I could feel their presence.

I am not one for sentimentality. I do not believe it does any good. It only makes one woozy with longing. The love in me that I felt when I returned to Omorfi was empowering. It reminded me of who I was that lead me to become who I am. No other place in Omorfi affected me as much as the beach I played on as a boy. As I got closer to it, I could smell and taste the salt water air, which tantalized my anticipation of my desired destination. I remember stepping on the sun beaten sand and it being hot. The vibrant sun was mightier than any cloud in the sky. The drifting clouds seemed to disappear in despair because they could not compete with the sun. I hurried through the grainy pebbled earth to the ocean's edge to relieve my feet's bottoms. The stark contrast of the hot sand to the cold water would tingle my feet, shoot up my legs, pass through my spine and flutter into my heart making me feel alive. The excitement of being at the beach was equally emotional and physical. I remember being fixated on the rhythmic waves and moment by moment, they would rush on to the shore gently covering and refreshing my feet. The waves would console me - "Shhh… Shhh… Shhh" is what they would say - reassuring me that all is good. I stood there for a bit and watched the water approach me and then recede. Slowly, it would breathe in and just as it caught its breath, it would exhale with relentless consistency. Sometimes, the tide is high and sometimes, it is low, but I would never say that the ocean gets tired because it never stops. It never gives up. The ocean knows better than anyone that life is not a sprint. It is a marathon. It knows that tomorrow is another day. The ocean has been around longer than life itself and it marches on with confidence. I do not know what will happen tomorrow, but the ocean might. It is older, stronger and wiser than I am. I stood in front of the water and looked out to the ocean looking for answers and they came to me. My cares seemed to drift away with the wind. The ocean whispered to me reassuring me that all is not lost. It told me that there are things that I do not know, but that I should not lose faith. My heart murmured inside me, "meditation, meditation, meditation." I trust the ocean because it has never lied to me. Before I reached the ocean, my mind was in a fuss, but as I stood there gazing at and pondering into the triumphant ocean, it knew what to say to me to return my mind to peace. Day and night I see it in my mind's eye. As I approached it, it reminded me that it has answers. Nothing on earth is wiser than the ocean, but in all of Creation, nothing is wiser than the stars. They dwell in the heaven of heavens and shine bright reminding me of God's Eternity. I look up to them and like the ocean, they speak to me. The stars are kind, gentle and have never let me down. They do not run. They shine unapologetically. Even the ocean listens to the stars because the stars oversee it, too. I look up and the stars bring me to the edge of my thoughts encouraging me to find my own answers. The stars, tranquil and sublime, speak softly and humbly to me. Sometimes, I think I found the answers on my own, but when my troubles return, I know I must go to the stars who know me better than I know myself.

My aunt was not formally educated, but she understood the value of an academic education and encouraged me to pursue a university degree. She believed it is something that I would always have, something that no one could take away, something with undisputed value. She nourished an orphaned boy's body, mind and soul to good health and helped bring me closer to God. In many ways, I am who I am today because of my aunt. She gave me the opportunity to live a full life. Mike and Gabe, too, helped to define my life. They were fundamental to my recovery from my parents' deaths and still further, they enriched my life. They are an invaluable gift to me from God. My philia for them is limitless. I would lay down my life for them. After my parents' deaths, God blessed me with a new life and I thank Him every night in my prayers.

YOUNG EZEKIEL
A LIFE OF LOVES

THREE

EROS

After I graduated from high school, I attended a small private university near the valleys of Pennsylvania. I earned high grades in high school and was offered a full-tuition scholarship with room and board. I had never been as excited as I was the moment I read the words, "Congratulations! You have been accepted…" I began to experience the fruits of my labor and it felt good. A high school teacher told me in life, if you persevere, you will "make" things go your way. I was beginning to realize the truth in his words. Life is both art and sport and the more we put in to it, the greater the masterpiece. We just have to care about life to make our lives worth living.

When I moved to Pennsylvania, Mike and Gabe stayed in the Boston area. Mike became a carpenter's apprentice. He was good with his hands and was skilled with tools more so than with books. Gabe entered the culinary trade and started out by assisting a chef in a French bistro with the goal of becoming a chef himself. We each had different strengths and contributed to the world in different ways.

During my first semester at the university, I noticed a change in myself. I was growing up. My clothes were more adult and I was standing taller. I developed a stride. It was the brash swagger of a college kid who was discovering his potential, but who had not yet been tested by the world. It was a wonderful time and everything was new. It was unknown territory for me and I was ready to explore. Never shy as a youth, but, perhaps, a bit reserved, I made a conscious effort to make friends. I developed an outgoing spirit and became more gregarious. I was meeting new people and reading the works of some of the greatest thinkers of all time. When I was accepted to the university, I was undecided on what subject I wanted to study, so I entered the liberal arts program. I figured, by doing so, I would learn a little bit of everything. This passive decision turned out to be a blessing. In the program, we studied the most influential ideas and the greatest works of all time from the East and the West and from the humanities and natural sciences. I relished in my books and was most enchanted with philosophy. It was exhilarating to read 5th century BC Greek philosopher Plato's *The Republic* and I saw myself as a philosopher king. My mind was like a sponge in that I was absorbing all kinds of information from many directions sometimes with little discretion. The ideas of those influential

Western philosophers seemed most enlightening. More than once, I remember saying to myself, "Ah, yes. There it is. Now, I see. Here is truth," but I was naïve and impressionable. Philosophy at its best opens discussion. It rarely provides answers; rather, it provokes one to think more deeply and ask further questions. A professor of mine once told me that confusion is a good thing because it means you are still thinking. If you are no longer confused, it means you have stopped thinking and you should not be satisfied, but alarmed. For a while, I believed that. But, then, through life's trials and tribulations and some self-examination, I discovered truth in Jesus's words and I am no longer confused and I am at peace with that; moreover, I am happy.

The program was a stepping stone for me. It was the catalyst for a dazzling period in my life of thoughtful inquiry and desire for knowledge. It paved the way for greater intellectual expeditions later in life. The program accomplished what it intended to do, which was to open my mind to possibilities and shift my thinking from a parochial view to a world view, and I greatly appreciate it for that. It was essential to my learning development. But, when one discovers Jesus as the Christ, all other knowledge is unfulfilling. When one accepts Jesus as the Christ, the goal is no longer the acquisition of knowledge or anything else; rather, it is to be his loyal servant.

There are two philosophies about success in life: work for money or do what you love. Some people are blessed and they make money by doing what they love, but for most, it is a fork in the road. The world tells us, "Make money" and I want to tell the world, "I have dreams." In our world, money is a necessity - it is how we share resources - but money should not be the goal. There will never be enough money. If a person can find a passion, he must not let it go to make money - the risk of losing his passion is too great. So, at the university, I studied the liberal arts because that was the only material that I was excited about. I may not have developed a practical skill, but the knowledge that I acquired was an investment in myself.

I spent a lot of time in the school library. It gave me access to thousands of books for free. I could reference dozens of books without leaving the building. It made it easy to build, expand and focus my knowledge and compare histories, ideas and philosophies. I could jump from the Chinese dynasties to communist Russia, from classical Greece to modern Germany. I could explore at my own pace; sometimes in an excited frenzy and sometimes in deep hard contemplation. I was hungry for knowledge and at times, I wanted to physically consume the books as if, with every swallow, the answers would come to me more quickly. Some of the books were worn because of their popularity; while, others were covered in dust. On the shelves, every book was a coffin with words inside, but once one was opened, it found air and was given new life.

In each book, death and immortality fought every time a patron entered the library.

When I was not in the library, I was with my friends meeting girls and trying to figure them out. God knows my heart wanted to love, but my mind was poisoned with lust. Love and lust are not the same. Love comes from the soul, while lust is all physical. Love is about both people in the relationship, while lust is just about oneself. If one is only concerned with what one can get, the relationship between the couple is doomed. Lust has no positive attributes - it only corrupts male and female. It is fantasy and deception that is contrary to love. Fleeting and ultimately unfulfilling, lust is one of the greatest lies. Because of my sexual liaisons with the girls, my confidence grew and I thought of myself as a real man, but I was far from being a real man, I was far from God.

After graduation, I had a degree, but no job. I was filled with knowledge from my liberal arts classes and now I had to figure out how I was going to apply this knowledge. I knew finding my place in the world was going to take time, but I was following my heart and gut. I wanted more than money. I moved to a town next to Philadelphia and had some random jobs here and there, but my first substantial job was when I was twenty-three in a hospital. My mother was a nurse and I saw how important the profession was to her. I followed her lead because I, too, want to help those in need. Working there, I learned about life's dignity and value and I think there are few places where one can witness greater heights of life's dynamism. Life and death fill every corner of the quarters. I've seen babies enter the world and people leave the world. Every day there is celebration and mourning. Life is respected and God is reverenced in hospitals. The evil of disease is visible, but so, too, is the kindness of nurses. People are healed to good health. Modern medicine and technology thrive in hospitals and the ancient wisdom of doctors to "first do no harm" is practiced.

My job mainly consisted of filing documents, changing bed sheets and tending to patients. It was not a prestigious job, but I felt it was noble. I felt like I was making a difference, even if it was one patient at a time. My co-workers and I were a team with the goal of making our weak patients strong. There was a doctor in my unit who often carried *The Little Flowers of St Francis*. He wore his white coat and the book stuck out of his pocket, just enough, so I could make out the title. That image has stayed with me. He figured it out. He made the connection between healing the body and the soul. During the most troubling times, he was able to comfort his patients. I bought the same book the doctor had and during my down time, I did a little reading.

I was having a good time at work. Barry, my supervisor, was a good guy and in many ways, I considered him a friend. We were not true friends, but that's okay. The circumstances of our relationship prevented that. We were friends of utility. We had an agreement with certain expectations that had to be met for the relationship to last. As long as I worked hard for him and performed well at my job, he would allow me to continue to work for him. But, it was not only about business. We were also friends of pleasure. We talked sports and current affairs and our senses of humor were the same. The day would pass quickly when we worked together.

One of my favorite people at work was Olivia - the lady at the greeting desk in the lobby. We had the same work schedule. She was a heavy lady, very sociable and well liked. She was also a big basketball fan, like me. One morning, I walked into the hospital's lobby and she saw me and asked,

"Ezekiel, honey, did you see Michael Jordan last night?"

"I certainly did. He scored 49 points," I answered.

"He's a pleasure to watch. I look forward to Chicago Bulls games," she said.

"Who would you rather see win, the Philadelphia 76ers or the Chicago Bulls with Michael Jordan?" I asked.

"Ezekiel, honey, you know I am a Philly native, but I have to admit: I sometimes catch myself cheering for Michael Jordan. I just hope he takes it easy on my Sixers," she replied.

"I understand," I said with a chuckle.

Olivia was usually inundated with visitors, phones and messages, but that day we had a few minutes to catch up. It was her daughter's fourth birthday a few days before and she showed me some photos of the party. She purchased a piñata and she had a couple of great photos of her daughter and friends scrambling to collect the falling candy from the broken piñata. Catching up with Olivia was a good way to start the day, which would turn out to be a great day. I was busy and time seemed to be flying by. I did not even realize that I missed lunch. The unit was running like a well-oiled machine with everybody working together. There are few highs that are greater than when everyone is working together with each other for each other. However, time stopped when I noticed a beautiful girl sitting in the waiting room in my unit of the hospital. She looked great: hair flowing, good posture, legs crossed. She was a natural beauty with inviting features. Sitting there, she opened her bag, reached in and pulled out a book. She held it in front of her, flipped a few pages and began to read. "Perfect... I love books... there's my opening," I said to myself. "I'll just ask her what she is reading." So, I made like I was working and walked into the waiting room to tidy up the magazines, seats and pillows. Then, I walked over to the girl and as her eyes ran across the page, I asked,

"What are you reading?"

"Oh," she said, "*The Alchemist.*"

It was as if all the stars in the sky directed me to her at this moment in our lives at this point in history because *The Alchemist* was one of my favorite books.

"That's a great book," I said. "Where in the story are you?" I asked.

"Just the first few pages," she said.

"If you're a dreamer, you will like it. I'm a dreamer and I like it. It will inspire you to be what you always knew you should be. It's deep, but accessible. I've recommended it to friends. It will place you somewhere, but not here and will draw you in with mystical phrases like 'Personal Legend' and 'Soul of the World.' And, it's not too long, which is always a plus."

I looked into her eyes. She had beautiful eyes - pools of caramel. I could swim in her eyes. And, she welcomed me with her eyes - growing bigger and brighter.

"Sounds amazing," she said. "I look forward to reading it."

We both took a deep breath.

Then, I asked, "What's your name?"

"Julie," she answered. "And you are?"

"I'm Ezekiel."

"That's a unique name," she said.

"It's Hebrew. It means 'God strengthens,'" I said.

"I like names that mean something or represent something. The name Julie is not very interesting."

"I like it. It reminds me of Juliet and star-crossed love," I said.

"I guess so," she replied demurely.

We spoke for a bit and then her cousin entered the waiting room. The two came to the hospital because her cousin got into a bicycle accident. She was on the road training for a race when a car got a little too close. She got startled and fell to the ground. The doctor gave her some antibiotics for lacerations on her elbows and knees. She was pleasant, but was in some pain and wanted to head home.

Then, Julie said, "Well, it was nice to meet you."

"Same here," I replied.

"I'll see you around," she said.

As she was walking away, but before I lost my chance, I asked, "Hey, Julie. Would you like to get some coffee some time?"

"Sounds nice," she said with a smile.

Then, we exchanged phone numbers. I was cloud high. Few things are as exciting as making that first connection with a girl. In these moments, the unknown is thrilling. Anticipation becomes intoxicating and the imagination takes over. I gave her a call and we made plans to meet Friday after my shift at work ended. We were going to meet in the hospital's lobby and walk to the local coffee shop.

Friday finally arrived. I could barely wait to see her. All day at work I thought about her. I got a little nervous, but it was a good nervous because I felt alive. All my senses were rushing and when I saw her in the lobby, I felt like a gush of cool water washed over me. I saw her, she saw me and she smiled. That was all I needed - her smile lit me up.

We walked together down the road to the coffee shop. It was spring and there was a gentle breeze in the air. The sun was setting turning the sky into pale purple and pink. Feathery clouds caressed the sky, which was melting into the horizon. Beside the sidewalks, shrubs bloomed flowers and above, trees housed singing sparrows. It was a quiet neighborhood where bakers baked bread and window shopping was a pastime. People nodded hello and couples held hands. I was walking taller than usual with Julie by my side.

We entered the coffee shop, stepped to the counter and ordered drinks. I paid and then we took our drinks, found a table with a couple of seats, sat down and got to know each other. I learned that she liked art and I like art, so we talked art much of the night. The previous summer, she journeyed to Florence, Italy to visit family.

I said, "I hear Florence is amazing with its Renaissance history."

"It is," she replied. "In Florence, I saw Michelangelo's *David*. He's much taller than I expected, much taller than any man. He stands unaffected, self-assured and with poise. He's young, the age when he killed Goliath. I was awestruck knowing that he was once a block of cold marble stone, but Michelangelo brought him to life. Michelangelo saw his subjects in the marble and carved them to set them free. In the museum, along with the *David*, are Michelangelo's "unfinished slaves," which show the chisel to stone marks that illustrate his vision to release life within the living stone.

She was excited to share her experiences with me and I enjoyed listening.

She said, "We also stopped in Rome in Vatican City in Saint Peter's Basilica where there is one of Michelangelo's Pietas, which is powerful. It depicts a youthful Mother Mary - majestic and regal - as she cradles her lifeless son. She is sorrowful and in disbelief and with her hand's gesture, she says, "Look at my son. They have killed him." Her gesture also says, "Here he is. He has done it - that which he was meant to do." And, with her demeanor, she glorifies him. I never studied art formally, so I may sound naive, but Michelangelo's work spoke to me."

I said, "One day, I would like to see what you saw. Michelangelo was a genius and his masterpieces are divine. He may not be a saint, but I am sure his art has inspired saints."

She said, "I'm lucky, I know, to have seen these wonderful things. One day, I would like to go to Amsterdam in the Netherlands where there is the Vincent Van Gogh museum. You should come with me. Vincent Van Gogh is my favorite artist."

I added, "He's one of my favorites, too. Like Michelangelo, he was a genius, but his story is deeply dramatic and tragic. I read that even though he painted something like 900 paintings in 10 years, he sold only one in his lifetime. I also learned that he may have suffered from seizures and mental illness, which may be why he cut off his ear and shot himself in the chest killing himself. Some of my friends and I visited the Museum of Modern Art in New York City and got up close to *Starry Night*, which is unlike anything from any other painter."

We sipped our coffees and long after we were done, we stayed in the coffee shop talking. Our conversations were unhurried, effortless and free. Never was it an "interview" as if we were applying for jobs. Our conversations did not go back and forth as if we were playing tennis, which as conversation, can be repetitive and exhausting. I mentioned I liked her purple knit scarf and she told me that her student's mother made it for her because of her dedication to the young girl. Julie was a fourth grade teacher who was passionate about her job and was devoted to her students. It is meaningful work and I let her know. I told her my favorite teacher, when I was young, made me believe I could be great one day. As an adult, her voice stayed with me and she made me believe in myself. When I doubted myself or failed, I thought of her. The greatest adults help children see their potential. It is like planting seeds and strengthening roots. It worked for me and is something I pass on to those younger than me. Not once did Julie and I force our conversations or did they end up at dead ends. Sign posts appeared which turned into new topics. We were enjoying each other's company and the slight pauses added a playful tension that only heightened our attraction for each other. I learned she liked to sing. When she was little, she would sing to entertain her family during gatherings and holidays. She and her cousins would put on a show for the older generations and it became a tiny tradition for them and something they all looked forward to when they got together. I told her I sang, too, but only in the shower because the acoustics made my voice sound just right. She liked poetry and told me one night she performed at an open mic in a bar in Philadelphia. She said she was nervous, but excited. I told her I would love to hear her poetry, but she shied away suggesting that she wanted us to get to know each other better. I asked why she was shy if she could stand in front of a crowd of strangers. I would be just as welcoming as they were and she told me it was a possibility allowing the thought to marinate in my mind. We spoke about pop-culture and the inanity of certain celebrities and learned that we shared common opinions. I told her I liked her car. It was a Mini-Cooper. She told me it was her first new car purchase. Her previous car she inherited from her grandparents. Then, I told her about my first car, which was a 1988 Dodge 600 that had fuzzy dice hanging on the rearview mirror. At some point, the passenger door stopped opening and to sit in the passenger seat, my friends would have to jump through the open window. The car had character, to say the least. When Julie and I communicated, we listened to each other and did not just wait to talk. And, not once did either of us look at our watches or phones looking for the time waiting for the date to end. The only clue that revealed the passing of time was when the sun was setting and night was filling the air. The glistening stars were beginning to break through the dark sky. It was as if God scattered diamonds over the heavens and left them there so we could venerate His Glorious Creation. The lucid evening was transformed into a brilliant night while we were together in the humble coffee shop.

We walked back to the hospital and as we walked, we talked some more. Our steps gradually aligned in sequence as we walked side by side together as a pair. We reached our cars and said goodnight. Our first date could not have turned out better for a first date. The future looked good for me and Julie, but it was still too early to tell if my dreams would materialize.

After our first date, we were eager to reunite. We spoke on the phone every day when we were not together. I learned we lived not far from each other. A few days later on our second date, I picked her up at her apartment at around 8:30PM. I parked my car on the side of the street, walked to her doorstep, rang her doorbell and she answered. Seeing her again, I felt alive. I almost forgot what that felt like when I was not with her, but it came back in full force when I saw her. "Did my heart love till now?" (Shakespeare, *Romeo and Juliet*, 1.5.50). When she saw me, she smiled with her rose tinted cheeks and I smiled back. The night had begun and we were ready to celebrate because we were together, again.

Her apartment was about twenty minutes away from our destination, a suburb near Philadelphia. It was a quaint town that by day, was mild tempered, but by night, its Main Street was hopping with energy. There were about a dozen bars and restaurants on that street that catered to young adults, like us. Each establishment pulsated with rhythms and melodies that snuck out of each entrance, that teased the people outside to step inside, that invited patrons to join the party. The atmosphere was fun and it was an environment that was hard to dislike. The spring air was crisp, far from humid. People wore jeans. The young men casually wore collar shirts and the young women wore scarves around their necks, draped over their shoulders. I parked my car, we crossed the road and walked together down Main Street to the bar I chose for the night. I opened the door and we were greeted by a doorman. He was a friend of mine and let us in without charging us an entrance fee. We walked in and the lights were dim and the place was filled with people - talking, laughing and dancing. I noticed a couple of unoccupied bar stools, so I held her by the hand and we navigated through the sea of people to claim our seats. A band was playing that night which is why I chose the venue. Live music always enhances the vibe in a bar and the band that night was talented which made the night even more special. We settled in and were enjoying the atmosphere. I bought myself a bottled beer and her a vodka gimlet. She told me she liked the place and I told her it was one of my favorite spots. Her incandescent smile was complemented with her subtle laugh and she styled herself with class that was elevated by her quiet confidence. As the evening passed by, our conversations got more playful. We sat shoulder to shoulder. During a moment of silence between us, I slid my hand down her arm, extended my fingers and grasped her hand and she grasped mine.

> If I profane with my unworthiest hand
> This holy shrine, the gentle sin is this:
> My lips, two blushing pilgrims, ready stand
> To smooth that rough touch with a tender kiss
> (Shakespeare, 1.5.91).

She turned her head toward me and I leaned in. Then, we kissed. Paused. And, then, we kissed, again. From that moment, I was hers and she was mine.

When we left the bar, the avenue was bustling with young adults, but we were one. We did not want to leave each other. Love is relentless and euphoric.

It is those moments of eros that we wish would last forever. There is no earthly high that is higher and it is not something that happens often. It takes the right person at the right time. I drove her to her home and we kissed goodnight. With that kiss, I felt complete. She stepped out of the car, walked to her door, unlocked it and entered safely. Then, I drove home in bliss.

The next time we got together, a few days later, I picked her up at her apartment and we went out for dinner. We decided to get sushi, so I took her to a Japanese restaurant that had a more traditional atmosphere than most. When we walked in, near the entrance, there was a rock fountain and a few bonsai trees. We were greeted by the hostess and took off our shoes. The hostess guided us to our dining area, which was enclosed by white screens. This allowed for privacy from the other patrons in the large open room. Some of the screens were decorated with calligraphy and along the walls were prints of nature scenes like mountains, trees and waterfalls. At the center of our dining area was a table that was near to the ground because there were no chairs. Instead, there were mats and we sat with bent knees on our legs. Our server handed us moist towels to wash our hands. We began with a bowl of edamame. Then, we each ordered two sushi rolls with a miso soup and green tea. The restaurant was quiet, not because it was empty, but because everyone spoke softly and so, we did, as well. It was different than most Western restaurants, which made the experience fun. After dinner, I took her to a small family-owned cafe that was known for its homemade cheese-cake. We had dessert and some coffee, but the night was young and we did not want it to end, so we went to my apartment.

We walked up a few steps and entered through the front door. In my living room, there was a black couch and a couple of black seats that sat around a rectangular dark brown wooden coffee table. There was a window with a large plant beside it and hanging on the walls were some prints. Pictures rested on top of end tables. I gave her a tour of my apartment and then we walked back into the living room. I asked her if she wanted something to drink and she asked for a glass of water. I served her water with some ice and a lemon wedge. In the living room was my vinyl record collection. I like jazz music, so I put on John Coltrane's *Stellar Regions*. I clued her in to the artists and the various genres. We sat on the floor listening to music and telling stories. She hummed as she thought and such endearing intimacies made me feel like we had known each other forever. They are intimacies that not everyone gets a glimpse of or could appreciate, little things, like a gesture or look, that make eros special. During a moment of silence, she got up and walked over to the music shelves to check out my records. Then, she walked around the room to get a closer look at the pictures.

"Is that you?" she asked.

I walked over to her and looked at the picture that she was pointing to and said, "Yes, it was."

"You were cute," she said with a smile.

"And, that must be your mom. She was beautiful. And, your dad - he looks like a proud papa," she said.

"They were great people," I said.

"What do you mean 'were?'" she asked.

"When I was twelve, my parents died in a car accident. A reckless college girl was drinking that night and hit my parents from behind. My parents' car swerved into oncoming traffic and hit a truck and they died instantly. I loved them very much. They were all I knew and their love remains with me every day."

"Oh my, I did not mean to pry," she said.

"I do not mind," I said. "I like talking about them. I do not get to talk about them much. It feels good when I do because it helps me to remember. It makes me feel like they are still alive."

I told her about Omorfi and how we lived by the beach, how father was a high school history teacher and how father, mother and I would sing songs on Saturday mornings. I told her about all the storge we had for each other.

Then, I said, "When my parents' lives ended, so did mine, but my aunt stepped in and adopted me and provided me with a new life. She nurtured my body, mind and soul into good health. I've been through a lot, but I'm still here. I'm a survivor."

She looked me in the eye and I could feel her love.

She said, "I'm sorry, Ezekiel, that you had to go through all that. The world is a difficult place. Some days, I believe I have found Heaven here on earth and other times, I question if Hell could be worse. Life can be unfair. I know. When I was eleven, my father was diagnosed with brain cancer. He was a sincere man who lived for his family and always had a loving disposition. Slowly, he lost mobility, then speech, then his ability to respond to our presence. The cancer was killing him and stealing his life from us. He fought for three years and then God freed him from his battle and he left this world when he was only forty-one and I was only fourteen. But, I have faith and I believe that when my journey here on earth ends, I will be with my father, again, in Paradise with God where there is no more pain and life is everlasting. Some days are tougher than others, but I believe the love of those close to us has the power to heal and I realize, more than ever, how delicate, tender and special life is. I'm so happy I found you. My days with you are pure joy and I thank God that you are in my life. I have never been as happy as I have been with you. I have never felt this way before."

Then, I said, "I am no merchant of the sea, yet wert thou as far as that vast shore washed with the farthest sea, I should adventure for such merchandise as you" (Shakespeare, 2.2.81).

Then, she said, "My kindness is as boundless as the sea, my love as deep; the more I give to thee, the more I have, for both are infinite" (Shakespeare, 2.2.132).

For the rest of the night, we said no more. We gazed into each other's eyes and stayed up kissing and caressing. Then, we fell asleep in each other's arms. The next morning, Julie woke me up with a kiss and she told me that she loved me and I told her that I loved her. It was a perfect moment.

My relationship with Julie was my first real romantic relationship. It was the first time I experienced the love form eros, which is the Greek term for romantic love.

I was in love with Julie, in eros with her, but my feelings for her were more than sexual. We are more than animals. She was not just a body. She was a soul. Certainly, I desired sex, but more than that, I desired her, her presence, her love. I fell for her and she fell for me. I could see it in her eyes, feel it in her touch, hear it in her voice, taste it in her kiss and smell it in her perfume. We communicated on multiple levels and we had our own world. When I was with her, I did not want be with any other girl. She was all I wanted. All I wanted was her and I wanted her to feel the same way about me. I would have done anything for her, not just so she would reciprocate my love, but so she, too, could genuinely experience eros and feel what I felt because it felt so good.

It was as if I knew Julie before we met and when I met her, it was as if we were reuniting. But, at the same time, everything was new and fresh. With her, a new chapter in my life began, an exciting, ecstatic and exhilarating chapter. I did things with Julie that before her, I never would. I love the melodies and rhythms of music, but I was uncomfortable with dancing. Julie got me to dance with her when we were alone and sometimes when we were in public. She brought out a different side of me. She helped me grow. She was beautiful on the outside and in the inside. She caught my attention because of her looks, but I fell in love with her because of her soul. I considered her a friend because we saw things in the same way, walked the same path and shared a common vision. We were friends, not in the way that I considered Mike and Gabe friends - sexual attraction and tension prevented that - but I considered her my equal. Julie and I were a pair, a couple, partners in a way that only a man and woman can be. We complemented each other and were a match.

The first time Mike and Gabe met Julie was when Julie and I visited Massachusetts. Julie and I had been dating for about a year, so I must have been twenty-five. While I was studying and then working in Pennsylvania, I would return to Massachusetts during summers and holidays because it was my home and to see my aunt, Mike and Gabe. This time, I returned when it was Memorial Day weekend and

Julie and I stayed at my aunt's house. Mike and Gabe had apartments not far from where we grew up. On that Saturday night, we decided to go to a bar that Mike, Gabe and I frequented when I would return home. It had over twenty beers on tap, which were backed up by over sixty different bottled beers. We sat at the corner table and ordered a bunch of appetizers - no meals, just a sampling of the house specialties. Julie was a natural fit into our crew. She quickly picked up our sense of humor. They each told stories about me pushing my comfort zone and keeping me on the edge of my seat. However, because they loved me, they also told stories that elevated me to royalty status, even hero status. We spent hours together and talked about the past, present and future, about politics, principles and popular culture. We had fun and laughed a lot. It was like the best party with the best company. I remember looking at Julie and thinking to myself how lucky I was to have her as my woman. I was deeply in eros with her and when I looked into her eyes, I saw the world and myself and everything made sense.

In Greek mythology, Eros is the god of love. He appears in different forms in history. He is first identified as one of the primordial cosmic gods who was there at the beginning of time as an agent of procreation. The 700 BC Greek poet Hesiod refers to him in his *Theogony*, meaning "Birth of the Gods:"

Verily at the first Chaos came to be, but next

wide-bosomed Earth, the ever-sure
foundations of all the deathless ones who hold
the peaks of snowy Olympus, and dim
Tartarus in the depth of the wide-pathed Earth,
and Eros (Love), fairest among the deathless
gods, who unnerves the limbs and overcomes
the mind and wise counsels of all gods and all
men within them (2.116).
(Translation H.G. Evelyn-White
[http://www.greekmythology.com])

When I was with Julie, I was unnerved and
overcome with eros and she was the center of my
universe; nothing else mattered when I was with her.
Time and responsibilities disappeared and all that
remained was our eros. Later on in *Theogony*, Eros
and Desire are with goddess Aphrodite at her birth.
Aphrodite is also known as Venus and the scene of
her birth is famously depicted in Sandro Botticelli's
Renaissance painting.

In later mythology, Eros was depicted as
goddess Aphrodite's mischievous young winged son
who, with his bow and arrows and flaming torch, sets
the hearts of gods and men on fire with passion.
Today, we know this Eros as Cupid and see him
commercially on Valentine's Day gift cards.

There is also a story of Eros who, as a young
deity, falls in love with Psyche who falls in love with
him. Love falls in love and is loved. The tale was
first penned by Latin philosophical writer Apuleius

during the 2nd century AD, but as far back as 4th century BC, it appeared in Greek folklore and popular art. It is one of the most famous love stories in classical antiquity and it remains influential. It is echoed in fairy tales, such as *Cinderella* and *Beauty and the Beast*. In Greek, "eros" means love and "psyche" means soul. When I learned this, the story of Eros and Psyche became more interesting and I wanted to see if I could learn anything about the relationship between love and the soul.

I asked myself, "What can I learn from Psyche, if psyche means soul?" The story tells us that Psyche was the most beautiful women on earth. Words could not describe her radiance. Many people believed that she was not of this world and prayed to her, worshiped her and compared her to goddess Aphrodite. Can we say that all souls are as beautiful? Can we say that all souls can be mistaken for the divine? I believe so.

When the tale begins, Psyche longed and waited for love. Because of her radiant beauty, men did not approach her and she feared that her dreams of love would never be anything more than dreams. She woefully sat at home all alone weeping in despair because she wanted to love, be in love and be loved. Can we say the same is true for every soul? Do all souls long for love? Do all souls search for love? I think so. I think all souls desire love.

When Eros left Psyche and the two were separated, Psyche vowed to herself that she would do anything to get him back. She endured the trial of the mixed seeds, the trial of the golden wool, the trial of the black waterfall and the trial of the box in Hades. Can we say that all souls will do anything for love? Can we say that all souls will confront all challenges for love? I am not sure, but I know that at the peak of my relationship with Julie, I did not want to let her go and if we were separated, I would have done anything to get her back. I would have done anything for her love.

At the end, when Eros and Psyche were reunited, Eros took Psyche to heaven. All the gods were with them and there was a great banquet with savory foods, flowing wine, fragrant flowers and angelic music. Can we say that love takes all souls to heaven? Can love bring all souls closer to the gods? I do not know, but I will tell you that at the peak of my relationship with Julie, we felt as though we were experiencing heaven on earth and with her, I felt as though I was bursting with great light. We felt as though we were living in a timeless realm.

For a while, Julie and I thought we would be together forever - even after death because not even death could separate us and our love for each other. We thought mighty Eros would keep his promise to be with us forever. At his highest, in many ways, he was our god. Eros took over and everything we did, all the time we spent and every thought we had revolved around Eros. It was like a religion that we followed. We followed his rules, so he would bring us joy and we followed his rules out of fear, so as to not disrupt him. We were helpless to the powers of Eros. Who are we to deny the god of love? Eros invites us and teases us to join him and for some, it can do more harm than good, it can go wrong. But, for Julie and I, Eros was heavenly. The god of love was good to us. However, the magnitude of his initial impact did not last. Ironically, "he is notoriously the most mortal of our loves" (Lewis, 113). When Eros's power faded, we became disenchanted with him and each other. Julie and I were not able to stay together without Eros. We tried, but we were young and not able to handle our eros's descent. Little issues grew to become big issues. Then, we spoke about marriage and children. I did not want children. I gave it tremendous thought. Because of the pain I experienced and ugliness I saw in the world, I loved my children so much to not have them. I understood how hard life can be and the great responsibility and duty to be a good parent, which is the hardest and most important job in the world. I did not want to take that risk and fail my children and the world with that most serious task. Then, I asked myself, "If I did decide to have children, would it be for myself or for them?" Something that has to be considered. After that, we realized that we did not see our futures in the same way, so we broke up.

The eros I felt for Julie surpasses the eros I felt for any other female in my life. After Julie, I questioned if I would ever find a better woman. I had more love for Julie than lust. Eros is tricky and complicated in that way. Lust plays a role. It is seductive, like an intoxicating drug or potion. If another woman entered my life, I knew it would have to be because of love and not based on lust. Real men do not lust after women. They have agape love for them as handmaids of God.

YOUNG EZEKIEL
A LIFE OF LOVES

FOUR

AGAPE

By this we know love [agape], that he [Jesus] laid
down his life for us.
(1 John 3:16)

One Friday - specifically, Christian Great
Friday - I was working in the hospital's emergency
room. It was an unusually quiet day in my unit, so I
volunteered to work in the ER in case the staff there
needed help. It was understaffed because a few
people took off from work to go to church. I planned
to go to church, too, but not until late at night.

After the sun had set, the paramedics rushed
in with an old man on a stretcher. The old man was
wearing a brown suit and his white dress shirt was
saturated in blood. The nurses hurried to get to him
and evaluate his condition. Skin the color of bronze
and body tall and thin, he had full head of white hair
that was in disarray. He had a grimace on his face
and after each inhale of air, he held his breath trying

to block the pain he felt from his wound. The nurses called the doctor and pointed out what they noticed. The doctor examined the old man. As he made his assessments, he was calm, but intensely focused. Then, they entered the operating room. At the time, I was stocking up and organizing medical supplies, so they would be easy to get to and ready for when needed. I was working in the background supporting the nurses and doctors, so they could save lives. A bit later, the old man was brought out from the operating room. No longer in his suit, he was clothed in a blue gown with his right side bound up. He was incapacitated in an anesthetic slumber. He laid silently in recovery for a couple of hours and then started to groan in his sleep, but was unresponsive to outside stimuli. Three hours after surgery, he woke up. Drowsy, but awake, he rolled around a bit in his stretcher wanting to sit up, but unable. One of the nurses approached him, held his hand, supported his shoulder and said, "Take it easy, friend." He calmed down, then sighed. I asked the nurse if there was anything I could do for him and she said I can stay with him and tend to him. Not sure how to help, but eager, I let him know I was there,

"Hello, sir," I said softly.

With murky eyes, he mumbled, "Oh my, where am I?"

"You are in a hospital, sir," I said.

Stroking his gaunt face with his heavy hand, he was slowly putting the pieces together and making sense of his current situation.

"How are you feeling, sir?" I asked.

"Not well," he answered.

"Is there anything I can do for you?" I asked.

"I thirst," he said.

I walked away and then returned with some water in a paper cup and a straw. I held the water in front of him and he grasped my hand and sipped the water. After each swallow, he cleared his congested throat. When he let go of my hand, I took away the half-empty cup. Then, he dropped his head back onto the pillow and fell back asleep. He was exhausted. He fell in and out of consciousness for a while and finally awoke alert. He rubbed his eyes with his hand, took a deep breath and adjusted his position in the bed. I helped him. After he was settled, I gave him water, again, and as he drank, I could see it satisfied him. After each mouthful, he sat there and looked at the cup. After his final gulp, he said, "Nothing replenishes like water."

"Yes, sir," I said.

Then, he said, "Did you know, my young friend, that the human body is predominantly made of water? Depending on build, a person's body is between 50 to 70% water."

"Sounds familiar, sir," I said.

"I always found that fascinating," he said slowly. "Life is filled with fascinating facts. I have learned many things in my many years on this earth. I have been blessed. God has been good to me.

What we old people say about good health is true. It is more valuable than money, fame or any pleasure. And, the older you become, the more clearly you will see the truth of this insight. I have had many healthy years - more than most - however, I am afraid that my remaining moments here on earth are few."

His side hurt. He tried to lift his arm to test his body's limits and could not and then he shouted in pain. A nurse heard him and walked over. She checked his vital signs, but there was little more she could do for him. She adjusted his blanket, clasped his shoulder and then walked away. He started to cough and after each cough, he cleared his throat. We sat together for a moment in silence. I could see that the old man was thinking and reflecting.

After some time, he shook his head and said, "It all happened so quickly."

"What's that, sir?" I asked.

"The way I was shot on my way to church to celebrate Great Friday," he answered.

Great Friday is the most solemn and poignant day of the year for Christians. It is the day we commemorate Jesus's crucifixion and death. He was killed like a guilty criminal, but the Cross is a symbol of victory. Our reasoning minds tell us the way Jesus died is a curse and a disgrace; however, over two billion people wear the Cross around their necks with pride because Jesus was killed on the Cross for us because of his agape for us. Easter may be the most sublime and reverent day of the year because it is a day of hope and promise that there is eternal life with God in Heaven and that one day our bodies will resurrect. However, we love Jesus not for what he can give us, but because of his incomprehensible agape for us. His self-sacrificial death defines agape and he is worthy of adoration and adulation. The Cross is a sign of victory because on it, Jesus completed his mission for our salvation. Not even death could stop Jesus from fulfilling his mission. In fact, death made it possible. Dying for us is why he came into the world.

"How did it happen, sir?" I asked.

He explained, "The day started off well. I was in good spirits all day and all week because this year all Christians are celebrating Holy Week together and are going to celebrate Easter on the same day. This happens only every few years and it brings me great joy when the Christian community is united in brotherhood. My house is an eight minute walk from the church. I know because I walk to it for every Sunday service. All day it had been very foggy, so I could not see very well. I was focusing on each one of my steps trying to break through the misty air. My glasses began to fog up and I was having a difficult time seeing through them. I removed them from my face and from my breast pocket, I took out a handkerchief to wipe them. Then, I heard a ruckus behind me, so I turned around quickly, got distracted and dropped my glasses. I was in front of the neighborhood liquor store, which has been robbed in the past. I'm rarely out at night because the area is not safe, but today, service was at night. Usually, I walk that route on Sunday mornings when it is quite and danger is asleep. I bent down to pick up my glasses and was pushed from the back. I heard yelling in the background and then a gunshot. My side was pierced by the bullet. The young man that shot me did not mean to. I know because he looked stunned after the gun fired. He looked me in the eye and froze. There was a moment between us and I told him, "I forgive you." He ran and then the owner of the liquor store ran to me and pressed my side. I felt pain and saw blood on his hand. He hollered to his son, who was working with him in the liquor store, and a little while later the ambulance found us."

Blood from his pierced side was coming through the bandage. I called a nurse and she quickly entered the old man's room to remedy the issue. I left them, so they could have some privacy as she rebound his torso with gauze. I could hear the old man grunting in pain. When she was finished, she told me I could go back inside his room. The old man saw the Cross around my neck, so he knew I was a Christian and asked,

"My young friend, have you been to church to celebrate Holy Week?"

"Yes, sir. I was able to attend most of the services," I said.

"How beautiful was Palm Sunday?" he asked.

"Very beautiful, sir, very beautiful," I

answered.

Palm Sunday is one of the most beautiful and moving days in the year for Christians. It commemorates Jesus's triumphal entry into Jerusalem trumpeting his arrival as our King, Savior and God. He enters the city sitting on a donkey announcing that he is the King that Jerusalem had been waiting for. Prophet Zechariah prophesied:

> Rejoice greatly, O daughter of Zion!
> Shout aloud, O daughter of Jerusalem!
> Lo, your king comes to you;
> triumphant and victorious is he,
> humble and riding on an ass,
> on a colt the foal of an ass (Zechariah 9:9).

The crowd that greeted Jesus glorified him shouting, "Hosanna! Blessed is he who comes in the name of the Lord! Blessed is the kingdom of our father David that is coming! Hosanna in the highest!" (Mark 11:9b). They spread palm tree branches on the ground and hailed him as their king.

When I was young and attended church with my aunt, we would make palm leaf Crosses the day before Palm Sunday. That was Saturday of Lazarus. After church services and a light brunch in the recreation hall, our church community would gather to split palm leaves into strips - thin enough so we could fold them into Crosses. I only did this once a year - every Saturday of Lazarus - and the first few took a little time to shape. I had to refresh my memory and once it came back to me, I would make dozens of palm leaf Crosses, which would be handed to the church parishioners the next day on Palm Sunday. I would keep the Cross I received all year - sometimes, more than a year - because I felt its holy power would bless me.

For Christians, Palm Sunday is a day to celebrate, but the days following Palm Sunday are sad because we know that our King will soon be killed. Jesus is better than a political king who can gain territory or peace for his subjects in this world. He is our King and Priest who can save us from death and give us eternal life. Most did not understand this at first. Not even Jesus's disciples were fully aware of his eternal power. Not until Jesus rose from the dead and appeared to his disciples, did they fully understand his power. Truly, his kingship is not of this world. Jesus's reign is in the Kingdom of God and not in a kingdom of man.

• Only through Jesus's suffering can we understand his kingship. As Prophet Isaiah prophesied,

> [God] will divide him a portion with the great,
> and he shall divide the spoil with the strong;
> because he poured out his soul to death,
> and was numbered with the transgressors
> (Isaiah 53:12).

Behold, my servant [God's servant] shall
prosper,
he shall be exalted and lifted up,
and shall be very high.
As many were astonished at him -
his appearance was so marred, beyond human
semblance,
and his form beyond that of the sons of men -
so shall he startle many nations;
kings shall shut their mouths because of him;
for that which has not been told them they
shall see,
and that which they have not heard they shall
understand (Isaiah 52:13).

This world's kings may be baffled by Jesus -
Isaiah's prophesied Suffering Servant of God - and
his resurrection and the miracles worked in his name
by the Holy Spirit, but for Christians, they are as real
as God's Kingdom of Heaven.

Jesus was and is the only perfect man. He is
the only true king. The rest of us are small. None of
us can compare. Many men think they are big, but
truth is the best we can be are servants of the Great
King Jesus. He was selfless and is the ultimate king
because he paid the ultimate price with his life for his
servants. All we have is our life in this world and
Jesus laid his down for us, so we could have a
meaningful life with God. He loved us so much,
which is why he is the greatest king and for those

who choose to serve the Great King, the reward is God's Kingdom of Heaven. There are many leaders - both good and bad - in the world, but Jesus is the only Christ and Son of God. He is the strongest man ever for no one else can be crucified as he was and retain his love for God the way he did with patience and grace. He is our Savior, who saves our souls from hell, death and eternal suffering. It is a sublime mystery that God chose to humble himself to become man - for Jesus truly was God. And, a still deeper tragic glory that he died, so we could have life. He entered this world to teach and show us the meaning of agape and since his advent, the world has never been the same. Glory to thee, our God, glory to thee.

After we settled in, the doctor came over to tell the old man about his condition. The bullet missed his organs, but his wound, nonetheless, would not stop bleeding. His future did not look good and the doctor asked the old man if there was any family he would like to call. The old man said he was a widower and he and his late wife never had children. His friends had all died. He was one of the last of his generation and his social sphere was limited to the church. He had no one, so I had great sympathy for him and decided to stay by his bedside so he would not be alone.

"Do you know why we call it Passion of the Christ, my young friend?" he asked.

"I believe so, sir. I think it refers to Jesus's zeal, love and devotion for God," I answered.

"I understand why you say that, my young friend. It is true: Jesus loved God, but that is not why we refer to it as his Passion. The word 'passion' comes from a Greek word meaning 'to suffer.' Do you understand suffering?" he asked.

"Yes, sir. It means to go through pain, to hurt, to feel close to death," I answered.

"You are right, my young friend, but do you understand the glory of suffering?" he asked.

"What do you mean, sir?" I asked.

The old man took a deep breath and exhaled slowly. His pain was barely manageable. His pierced side would not stop bleeding. Then, he said, "Suffering brings us closer to Jesus who suffered. With suffering, we have the honor of emulating Jesus. If he could endure his Cross, we can endure ours. Perhaps, this is my Cross. Though I am anxious about death, Jesus is near to me and I know God will never leave me. Because of Jesus, I understand suffering and I know that after death, I will find peace with God and Jesus in Paradise."

I realized that if the Son of God experienced suffering, we are not immune to it either. It is a part of life. When my parents died, God gave me strength. God and Jesus understand my pain because of the pain they experienced when Jesus died. The Son of God lowered himself to reach us, so when we die we can be elevated to be with him. One who suffers to death and believes in Jesus is not far from Paradise and everlasting life.

Pain and struggle add depth to the soul. Recovery is strength. Jesus makes recovery possible. He is Salvation. Few people know pain, struggle, recovery and Jesus better than Black Americans. Like the Jews, they were once slaves, but God and Jesus saved them and have saved us all. Black American Gospel music is one of the greatest gifts any people has given to the world. The best songs are as powerful as the Psalms and they overflow with agape. To the shock of some, Jesus was not a white European. In truth, he was a Jewish man of color born in Palestine. And, revered by most, Mary was a Jewish teen virgin of color who gave birth to God.

Jesus knew what he was getting into and the suffering that was ahead of him. This makes his agape more compelling than if he did not know because most people, if they knew, would have run. As Prophet Isaiah prophesied,

> He was oppressed, and he was afflicted,
> yet he opened not his mouth;
> like a lamb that is led to the slaughter,
> and like a sheep that before its shearers is
> dumb,
> so he opened not his mouth (Isaiah 53:7).

There are a few times when the Gospels say that Jesus prophesied his own death and how it would happen. For example, Jesus told his disciples,

"Behold, we are going up to Jerusalem, and everything that is written of the Son of man by the prophets will be accomplished. For he will be delivered to the Gentiles, and will be mocked and shamefully treated and spit upon; they will scourge him and kill him, and on the third day he will rise" (Luke 18:31b).

Even in agony, Jesus's faith in God his Father remained steadfast. In Gethsemane in anticipation of his "cup" of suffering and death, he "prayed more earnestly; and his sweat became like great drops of blood falling down upon the ground" (Luke 22:44). To God, he prayed, "Abba, Father, all things are possible to thee; remove this cup from me; yet not what I will, but what thou wilt" (Mark 14:36). He was obedient to God's will and submitted to God's power. He was God's perfect servant and a son who adored his Father.

When Jesus was questioned about who he was, even if it meant suffering, he fearlessly told the truth:

The high priest then questioned Jesus about his disciples and his teaching. Jesus answered him, "I have spoken openly to the world; I have always taught in synagogues and in the temple, where all Jews come together; I have said nothing secretly. Why do you ask me? Ask those who have heard me, what I said to them; they know what I said." When he had said this, one of the officers standing by struck Jesus with his hand, saying, "Is that how you answer the high priest?" Jesus answered him, "If I have spoken wrongly, bear witness to the wrong; but if I have spoken rightly, why do you strike me?" (John 18:19).

Still further:

Now the chief priests and the whole council sought false testimony against Jesus that they might put him to death, but they found none, though many false witnesses came forward. At last two came forward and said, "This fellow said, 'I am able to destroy the temple of God, and to build it in three days.'" And the high priest stood up and said, "Have you no answer to make? What is it that these men testify against you?" But Jesus was silent. And the high priest said to him, "I adjure you by the living God, tell us if you are the Christ, the Son of God." Jesus said to him, "You have said so. But I tell you, hereafter you will see the Son of man seated at the right hand of Power, and coming on the clouds of heaven." Then the high priest tore his robes, and said, "He has uttered blasphemy. Why do we still need witnesses? You have now heard his blasphemy. What is your judgment?" They answered, "He deserves death." Then they spat in his face, and struck him; and some slapped him, saying, "Prophesy to us, you Christ! Who is it that struck you?" (Matthew 26:59).

Jesus, my King, not only experienced physical pain for us, but was also belittled, mocked and disgraced for us:

Then the soldiers of the governor took Jesus into the praetorium, and they gathered the whole battalion before him. And they stripped him and put a scarlet robe upon him, and plaiting a crown of thorns they put it on his head, and put a reed in his right hand. And kneeling before him they mocked him, saying, "Hail, King of the Jews!" And they spat upon him, and took the reed and struck him on the head. And when they had mocked him, they stripped him of the robe, and put his own clothes on him, and led him away to crucify him (Matthew 27:27).

My King is the Son of the Most High, yet he was stepped on like dirt. He suffered many things for me. The soldiers spat on him. How could they spit on my King? He lowered himself for me. Who am I? I am little and he is great. A devoted servant would lay down his life for his king, but my King laid down his life for his servants. What have we done to deserve such grace? How can we repay him? The only way I know how to repay him is to emulate him. We must be willing to sacrifice ourselves for him and the brethren. They treated him less than a human being when in reality he was God. It makes no sense, but if you listen to his words, you will see he did it out of agape. He was disgraced, but that is why I glorify him.

The climax of Jesus's Passion was his crucifixion - an incomprehensible suffering where the sentenced one dies slowly. With his limbs nailed to and his body hanging from a wood, Jesus cried with a loud voice, "My God, my God, why hast thou forsaken me?" (Mark 15:34 and Matthew 27:46). It would be hard to find greater suffering - suffering so great that the Son of God is praying for mercy. However, Jesus never curses God or His authority. Knowing he was innocent and was sentenced unjustly to death, Jesus never separated himself from God. On the Cross, with a loud voice, Jesus cried out, "'Father, into thy hands I commit my spirit!' And having said this he breathed his last" (Luke 23:46). It was finished. Triumph. Jesus accomplished what he was meant to do. To his very end, he was a messenger of the truth and fulfilled his mission for the forgiveness of our sins, so we can have eternal life.

Patients came and were treated as the old man and I sat and spoke. In the ER, things were always in motion and each patient's problem was unique.

Doctors qualified conditions into categories, but no two cases were the same. Most of the night, the regular staff had things under control and they let me stay with the old man. They understood that it was important for me to be there for him. They could see that the old man needed to talk to keep himself alert and lift his spirit. All my other responsibilities could wait. The old man was my top priority.

"Do you know who is the Good Shepherd, my young friend?" he asked.

"Of course, sir. It's Jesus," I answered.

"Do you know why he is called the Good Shepherd?" he asked.

"Not exactly, sir," I answered.

"It's because he laid down his life for us, his flock," he explained.

The old man was referring to John's Gospel 10:11, where Jesus says, "I am the good shepherd. The good shepherd lays down his life for the sheep. He who is a hireling and not a shepherd, whose own the sheep are not, sees the wolf coming and leaves the sheep and flees; and the wolf snatches them and scatters them. He flees because he is a hireling and cares nothing for the sheep. I am the good shepherd; I know my own and my own know me, as the Father knows me and I know the Father; and I lay down my life for the sheep. And I have other sheep, that are not of this fold; I must bring them also, and they will heed my voice. So there shall be one flock, one shepherd. For this reason the Father loves me, because I lay down my life, that I may take it again. No one takes it from me, but I lay it down of my own accord. I have power to lay it down, and I have power to take it again; this charge I have received from my Father."

The old man told me, "My young friend, meditate on Prophet Isaiah's prophecy of the Christ known as the Suffering Servant prophecy. See how this passage, older than 500 BC, describes Jesus's life and death, his mission and glory. If you open your heart, you will see Jesus. He fulfills the call, role and prophecy. At the end of the prophecy, Isaiah explains that "he bore the sin of many, and made intercession for the transgressors" (53:12c). We are the transgressors - the sinners in this world - and are far from God, but Jesus interceded for us, so we can have a way to unite with God. Sinful man has no way of entering Heaven and uniting with God on his own. We are unworthy of God because we have rejected Him, as did our parents Adam and Eve, and have no way of making amends with Him. God and His Son Jesus knew this and made a plan to save us from our wicked ways that lead to hell, so we can be with God forever in Heaven. The plan was for perfect Jesus to die for us. He was the only worthy sacrifice to God to redeem sinful man. It hurts God and Jesus for Jesus to be tortured and killed, but they did so willingly to retain justice in a God centered universe. God's Justice required punishment for sin and Jesus took our place.

Surely he has borne our griefs
and carried our sorrows;
yet we esteemed him stricken,
smitten by God, and afflicted.
But he was wounded for our transgressions,
he was bruised for our iniquities;
upon him was the chastisement that made us
whole,
and with his stripes we are healed
(Isaiah 53:4).

Only perfect Jesus was a satisfactory substitution for humankind. "The LORD has laid on him the iniquity of us all" (Isaiah 53:6). He satisfied the debt due to God for human sin. "He makes himself an offering for sin" (Isaiah 53:10). His blood was "poured out for many for the forgiveness of sins" (Matthew 26:28). Jesus paid the price for our sins. As Paul explained, "You are not your own; you were bought at a price" (1 Corinthians 6:19b). We dishonor God, as did our parents Adam and Eve, with our sin of disobedience. Jesus makes reconciliation possible between God and us. He was perfectly obedient to God's will to the very end of his life. His obedience mends the rift of our disobedience. This is known as atonement, which refers to our redemption and salvation. "By his knowledge shall the righteous one, my servant, make many to be accounted righteous" (Isaiah 53:11). This was made possible because of God and Jesus's agape for us. God loved us because He sent us His Son and Jesus loved us because he sacrificed himself for us. The only way for us to show our love for God is to honor and believe in His Son. We must accept Jesus as our Savior to be put right with God. Jesus makes atonement possible. We just have to believe in him, live his message and emulate his love. If we do, we will live forever in Paradise with God and Jesus. As taught in John 3:16, "For God so loved the world that he gave his only Son, that whoever believes in him should not perish but have eternal life."

Everything the old man said was profound and it meant more to me than it would have at any other time because it was Great Friday when we commemorate Jesus's self-sacrificial death. I sat with him for hours and as the night passed by, I was getting anxious because I wanted to go to church. However, when the end of my shift arrived, I was compelled to stay with him and miss the church service. I could not leave him. The thought that entered my mind was that, perhaps, it was more important to be with the old man. God seemed to have brought us together. He had no family, but I was there. I felt like I had a duty to be there for him. As I let that thought linger, another thought entered my mind: maybe, the old man was here to help me. He opened my eyes to many mysteries about Jesus. I had never had conversations as deep with another person as I had with the old man. I can think of nowhere else where I would have learned as much about Jesus, his Passion and the meaning of agape.

A nurse joined us. He overheard the old man and I talking about Jesus throughout the night. The nurse was raised Muslim and confessed to us that Muslims do not believe it was Jesus who died on the Cross. They believe it was someone else that was just like Jesus, someone else God transformed to be exactly like Jesus put in Jesus's place. As I have grown older, this confession has left me uneasy because of the virulent forcefulness of radical Muslims who pledge allegiance to Muhammad and his revelations. I have asked myself, "How can it be that Muslims do not believe Jesus died on the Cross? For who professed his Sonship to God? Who was accused at the trials and then carried the Cross? Who did Mother Mary weep to? Who spoke to John on the Cross to care for his Virgin Mother?

The nurse knew what he knew because of Muhammad's Qur'an, which says,

> And their saying: Surely we have killed the Messiah, Isa [Jesus] son of Marium [Mary], the apostle of Allah; and they did not kill him nor did they crucify him, but it appeared to them so (like Isa) and most surely those who differ therein are only in a doubt about it; they have no knowledge respecting it, but only follow a conjecture, and they killed him not for sure.

Nay! Allah took him up to Himself; and Allah is Mighty, Wise.

(Qur'an, Surah 4, 157-158. Translation M.H. Shakir)

But, the details of Jesus's final hours and death are well documented. It is the most well documented period described in all four Gospels and one of the most well preserved events in human history. The death of the Christ can be difficult to fathom, but it is authentic. It does not agree with conventional human wisdom and can be difficult to make sense of, but it was instituted because of God's Providence and Wisdom. It is not an event that we may like or want to accept or be proud of unless we are seekers of truth. His role was prophesied in the Old Testament and he fulfilled it. Those who have examined the Jewish Scriptures know it and so do those who have seen his workings in the world. The Cross is fundamental. If Muhammad, the author of the Qur'an, was wrong about the fact of Jesus's death, how could he have claimed that God gave him the revelations of the Qur'an? God is Truth, so did Muhammad make up what he wrote? What else could he have feigned divine revelation of? This Muslims must confront for themselves. It is their only path to Salvation. I pray they see the truth for the saving of their souls and the souls of their children.

The most valuable thing we possess is our souls. If we ask ourselves, "What is the soul?" we can conclude that it is the divine part of us - still further, it is the agape in us. The soul is the only part of us that can make us immortal. And, if we ask ourselves, "How do we reach immortality?" the answer is Jesus Christ. Jesus is the only way to become immortal and attain eternal life because he fills us with agape and only those who are filled with agape can become one with God who is Agape. Immortality is union with God and that is only possible through agape. To be filled with agape, we have to be reborn in spirit with God's Son Jesus. We do not know agape or how to give agape until Jesus enters us. It begins with respect and recognition of his suffering. Consider his suffering and it will lead to empathy. Agape compelled him and his agape will fill you with agape. Then, you will understand that he was no ordinary man. He will transform your mind and heart. And, when you pay attention to his teachings, you will hear truth in his words. No man spoke like this man. No man died like this man. No man loved like this man. Reflect and embrace him and you will understand why we Christians call him God's Suffering Servant, the Christ and God's Son.

As the hours of Great Friday were coming to a close, I read out loud to the old man the Gospel accounts of Jesus's crucifixion. Then, the old man asked me to read Psalm 22. He told me, "My young friend, meditate on this psalm, which is often referred to as the Passion Psalm. When you read it, try to hear Jesus's suffering and agony when he prays in Gethsemane and when he is hanging on the Cross. As the perfect Jew, the Lord quotes it as he is dying. He was always teaching, even to his very end." The old man inhaled, exhaled, took another deep breath and then continued. "You will see Jesus's humanity as he suffers as a man, but you will also see his confidence in God as God's Son. He never separated himself from God and was always one with God. He has nowhere to go. God is all he has. He trusts in God who gives him strength before he falls apart. Jesus endured to show us that we have the power to endure and that we must endure. God was with Jesus and God will always and forever be with those who love Him."

> Psalm 22 (RSV)
> Plea for Deliverance from Suffering and Hostility
> To the choirmaster: according to The Hind of the Dawn. A Psalm of David.
>
> My God, my God, why hast thou forsaken me?
> Why art thou so far from helping me, from the words of my groaning?
> 2 O my God, I cry by day, but thou dost not answer;

and by night, but find no rest.

3 Yet thou art holy,

enthroned on the praises of Israel.

4 In thee our fathers trusted;

they trusted, and thou didst deliver them.

5 To thee they cried, and were saved;

in thee they trusted, and were not
disappointed.

6 But I am a worm, and no man;

scorned by men, and despised by the
people.

7 All who see me mock at me,

they make mouths at me, they wag their
heads;

8 "He committed his cause to the Lord; let
him deliver him,

let him rescue him, for he delights in him!"

9 Yet thou art he who took me from the
womb;

thou didst keep me safe upon my mother's
breasts.

10 Upon thee was I cast from my birth,

and since my mother bore me thou hast
been my God.

11 Be not far from me,

for trouble is near

and there is none to help.

12 Many bulls encompass me,

strong bulls of Bashan surround me;

13 they open wide their mouths at me,

like a ravening and roaring lion.

14 I am poured out like water,
    and all my bones are out of joint;
my heart is like wax,
    it is melted within my breast;

15 my strength is dried up like a potsherd,
    and my tongue cleaves to my jaws;
    thou dost lay me in the dust of death.

16 Yea, dogs are round about me;
    a company of evildoers encircle me;
    they have pierced[a] my hands and feet—

17 I can count all my bones—
    they stare and gloat over me;

18 they divide my garments among them,
    and for my raiment they cast lots.

19 But thou, O Lord, be not far off!
    O thou my help, hasten to my aid!

20 Deliver my soul from the sword,
    my life[b] from the power of the dog!

21 Save me from the mouth of the lion,
    my afflicted soul[c] from the horns of the
wild oxen!

22 I will tell of thy name to my brethren;
    in the midst of the congregation I will
praise thee:

23 You who fear the Lord, praise him!
    all you sons of Jacob, glorify him,
    and stand in awe of him, all you sons of
Israel!

24 For he has not despised or abhorred

the affliction of the afflicted;
and he has not hid his face from him,
> but has heard, when he cried to him.

25 From thee comes my praise in the great
congregation;
> my vows I will pay before those who fear
him.

26 The afflicted[d] shall eat and be satisfied;
> those who seek him shall praise the Lord!
> May your hearts live forever!

27 All the ends of the earth shall remember
> and turn to the Lord;
and all the families of the nations
> shall worship before him.[e]

28 For dominion belongs to the Lord,
> and he rules over the nations.

29 Yea, to him[f] shall all the proud of the
earth bow down;
> before him shall bow all who go down to
the dust,
> and he who cannot keep himself alive.

30 Posterity shall serve him;
> men shall tell of the Lord to the coming
generation,

31 and proclaim his deliverance to a people
yet unborn,
> that he has wrought it.

The old man's teaching about this psalm was the final
lesson he spoke to me. The psalm reveals the

author's inner struggle, turmoil and suffering. It begins with pain, is filled with deep faith and ends with reverence. I saw it in the old man and Jesus went through it. Jesus's Passion (or Suffering) cannot be separated from his love because it is proof of his love for God and us. We meant the world to Jesus which is why he left the world for us.

By the time it was 11:20 PM, the old man was drifting in and out of consciousness. Our conversations had deteriorated into occasional looks at each other. I could see that he was getting weak as his eyes rolled around behind his heavy eyelids. Sweat beaded above his brow, so I put a damp cloth on his forehead hoping that it would bring him some relief. Then, he started to shiver, so I got an extra blanket and tucked it around him. When his skin started to turn pale, I did not know what to do to ease his pain. I sat with him trying to comfort him as best as I could even if he did not know I was with him. I knew his end was approaching. Then, for a brief moment, his eyes opened and he took a deep breath. In a voice not much louder than a whisper, I heard him pray: "Into thy hands, O Lord, I commend my soul and my body. Do thou thyself bless me, have mercy upon me, and grant me life eternal. Amen." Then, just before midnight, the last minute of Great Friday, he stopped breathing, his heart monitor flat lined and he departed from this world. I had never seen anyone die before and I had mixed feelings about the old man's death. I can best describe my feelings as a joyful sadness - sad because he died, but joyful because I knew he was with God and Jesus in Paradise.

For me, Great Friday is normally emotionally heavy because I mourn Jesus's death. However, witnessing the old man die on Great Friday, I developed a deeper understanding about death that was transformed from a scene that I saw in pictures and film into a raw and permanent reality. This man lived and died as did Jesus. Being with the old man during his final hours helped me to better know Jesus during his final hours. The next day, my spirit still felt heavy, but when I was in church that night for the Easter vigil, God strengthened me. Like fresh air into empty lungs, my spirit was rejuvenated because with my fellow Christians, I was celebrating Jesus's resurrection. In the dark church at the moment of midnight when it became Easter Sunday, the priest came out of the altar with the Sacred Light lit on candles and passed it to the congregation. From one candle to the next, the once dark church was filled with light and light overcame darkness, just as Jesus has overcome death. For we Christians, Jesus's death is the saddest day of the year, but his resurrection is the most joyous. From the moment of the Sacred Light for the next forty days, we Orthodox Christians greet each other with "Christ is Risen!" and respond with "Truly, He is Risen!" I wait all year to proclaim this truth with my fellow Christians. By rising from the dead, Jesus has destroyed Death.